W9-BVZ-157

Barbara Cartland

The **Prude** and the **Prodigal**

G.K. Hall & Co. • **Chivers Press**
Waterville, Maine USA   Bath, England

This Large Print edition is published by G.K. Hall & Co., USA and by Chivers Press, England.

Published in 2001 in the U.S. by arrangement with International Book Marketing Limited.

Published in 2001 in the U.K. by arrangement with Cartland Promotions.

U.S. Softcover   0-7838-9519-4 (Paperback Series Edition)
U.K. Hardcover   0-7540-4629-X (Chivers Large Print)
U.K. Softcover   0-7540-4630-3 (Camden Large Print)

The Prude and the Prodigal, copyright © 1980 by Barbara Cartland.

All rights reserved.

The text of this Large Print edition is unabridged.
Other aspects of the book may vary from the original edition.

Set in 16 pt. Plantin by Al Chase.

Printed in the United States on permanent paper.

British Library Cataloguing-in-Publication Data available

Library of Congress Cataloging-in-Publication Data

Cartland, Barbara, 1902–
    The prude and the prodigal / Barbara Cartland.
      p.   cm.
    ISBN 0-7838-9519-4 (lg. print : sc : alk. paper)
    1. Large type books.   I. Title.
  PR6005.A765 P78 2001
  823′.912—dc21   2001024783

Author's Note

Inigo Jones, 1573–1652, was the founder of the English classical school of Architecture. He visited Italy and attracted the patronage of Christian IV of Denmark, whose sister was married to James I of England.

Jones's greatest surviving buildings are the Banqueting Hall in Whitehall, the Queen's House at Greenwich, the Queen's Chapel in St. James's Palace, and the restoration of St. Paul's Cathedral.

Sir Anthony Van Dyke, 1599–1641, was, after Rubens, the most prominent Flemish painter of the Seventeenth Century. His enduring fame is for his portraits. He idolized his models without sacrificing any of their individuality. Their beautiful hands are characteristic of a genius.

NEWARK PUBLIC LIBRARY
NEWARK, OHIO 43055-5087

Large Print Car
Cartland, Barbara, 1902-
The prude and the prodigal
6894738

NEWARK PUBLIC LIBRARY
NEWARK, OHIO 43055-8087

Chapter One

1817

Prunella awoke and instantly began to think about Nanette.

Usually in the time between waking and being called she said her prayers, but this morning it was as if the problem which had been in her mind when she went to sleep was waiting for her like a ghoul sitting on the end of her bed.

"What am I to do?" she asked herself, feeling that she had tried everything already.

It had seemed such a good idea that Nanette, who was so pretty and so intelligent, should be presented at Court when she was seventeen.

Many of the girls in Society made their debut at that age, and as the mourning for their father had ended in March, it seemed almost like fate when Lady Carnworth, who was Nanette's Godmother, wrote and suggested that she should present her goddaughter to the Queen at Buckingham Palace at the end of April.

That gave them time, Prunella had calculated quickly, for Nanette to buy the elegant gowns that were essential for the London Season and to gain a few weeks' sophisticated poise before she actually made her curtsey.

Therefore, with complete confidence,

Prunella had accepted Lady Carnworth's kind invitation and had sent Nanette to London with a lady's-maid and an experienced Courier.

"I cannot think why you do not take me yourself," Nanette had said.

Actually the idea had never occurred to Prunella, but when Nanette suggested it she knew that Lady Carnworth would not want to chaperone two girls, and besides, Prunella had missed her chance years earlier.

"I am much too old," she had replied, her smile taking the sting from the words.

"Of course you are not!" Nanette had said loyally.

But she had not referred to it again, and Prunella knew she was a little embarrassed when she thought of how dull and dreary her elder sister's life had been these past three years.

Prunella, however, was not thinking of herself at the moment but of Nanette.

She had returned home the second week in June, after the Regent had left Carlton House for Brighton and the Season had to all intents and purposes come to an end.

"You must tell me everything, dearest," Prunella had said the first evening of her return.

Although Nanette had chattered away, she knew her sister well enough to suspect that something was being kept back.

It was soon obvious what that was, because even before Nanette had confessed — if that was the right word — Lady Carnworth wrote to Prunella:

There is no need for me to tell you that Nanette has been an unqualified success. Everybody was delighted with her looks, her gowns, for which I am prepared to take full credit, and of course for her sweet nature and exquisite good manners.

I am not going to pretend to you, Prunella, that the fact that she is an heiress did not smooth the way and open the doors for her to receive many invitations she might otherwise not have received. But of course, a young woman with money is bound to encounter difficulties, and the one I am going to tell you about, of course in confidence, is called Pascoe Lowes. He is the son of Lord Lowestoft and has been spoilt all his life by a doting mother and the fact that he is far too good-looking for any young girl's peace of mind.

When he attached himself to Nanette, my heart sank and I did everything in my power to put him off and to make her understand that he is well known as a "fortune-hunter" and therefore is a most undesirable parti in every way.

I am only hoping that now Nanette has left London and returned to the country, he will forget about her, and I thought it my duty to warn you that he has been very attentive and Nanette has, I am afraid, in consequence turned a cold shoulder on two quite suitable gentlemen who would, I am certain, had they been encouraged, have offered for her.

You must forgive me, dear Prunella, for not having somehow prevented this situation from arising, although I do not know what else I could have done to keep them apart once they had met.

I feel sure when you talk to Nanette you will make her see sense and that she can do far better for herself than to waste her time with Pascoe Lowes.

Prunella read the letter over and over again, and then wisely, because she loved her sister, waited until Nanette was ready to confide in her.

It was something she was eventually obliged to do, when a Post-Chaise arrived from London containing a huge bouquet of flowers and a letter.

Naturally Nanette had been excited by such an extravagant and flamboyant gesture.

"Can you imagine him sending flowers such a long way?" she had asked.

"Your admirer must be very rich!" Prunella had remarked.

Then, of course, the story came out.

"Godmama says that Pascoe is a fortune-hunter," Nanette related, "but it is untrue. He told me quite frankly he has no money, and he would have loved me even if I had not a penny to my name."

"But, dearest, you are in fact very rich," Prunella said, "and I cannot help thinking it would be a great mistake to marry a man without money."

"He will be able to spend mine," Nanette replied.

"If he was a decent man he would feel embarrassed at being in such a position," Prunella said firmly.

She talked quietly and eloquently on the subject, until she realised that Nanette was not listening but was looking with glowing eyes at the huge bouquet of flowers and touching the letter that had come with them, which was tucked into the sash of her gown.

A week later the Honourable Pascoe Lowes arrived to stay in a house about five miles away.

Prunella was surprised that he knew people in the area, until she suddenly remembered that his mother was the elder daughter of the late Earl of Winslow.

"I took no notice of his name," she said to herself, "but now I recall that Lady Anne married Lord Lowestoft, whose family name is Lowes. It was stupid of me not to remember it."

When she thought back she remembered hearing the Earl, who had been a great friend of her father's, say how boring he found his son-in-law, with the result that Lord and Lady Lowestoft seldom stayed at the Hall.

Prunella supposed they must have done so when she was a child, but later she had heard that Lord Lowestoft was bed-ridden, and of course during the war the Earl seldom entertained and her father appeared to be his only guest.

'It is a pity the Earl is not alive today,' Prunella thought when she learnt about Nanette's interest in his grandson.

She was quite certain that the old Earl, a fierce and rather terrifying old man, would not have allowed his grandson to behave in any way which was unbecoming to a gentleman. And what, indeed, could be worse than to be branded as a "fortune-hunter"?

When Pascoe Lowes was announced, Prunella saw at first glance that it was going to be difficult to persuade Nanette that he was only an extremely handsome, if overdressed, young man.

Prunella had never visited London and had therefore no idea of what the Bucks, Beaux, and Dandies actually looked like, but here was a man who was undoubtedly all three, walking towards her and to her eyes looking so fantastic that she felt she must be gaping at him with her mouth open like a goldfish.

"I am so delighted to make your acquaintance, Miss Broughton," this vision of elegance was saying. "Your sister has extolled your beauty and your virtues until I found it hard to believe that such a paragon really existed, and yet I see she has not exaggerated."

'He certainly puts on an excellent performance,' Prunella thought.

But at the same time the Honourable Pascoe spoke with such apparent sincerity and undoubted charm that despite herself she found she was smiling at his compliment.

He obviously was not listening to what she said, but was watching Nanette, and there was no doubt that he was looking at her in a meaningful and ardent manner which Prunella felt would turn the head of any girl, especially one as inexperienced as her sister.

By the time the visit was over, and the Honourable Pascoe was clever enough to make it short, Prunella was really alarmed.

He was, she was quite certain, everything that she would dislike in a brother-in-law and she felt that he would make Nanette extremely unhappy.

How could any girl who was country-bred tolerate a husband who must spend hours having his cravat tied in such a difficult, intricate fashion just to make all the other Dandies envious?

The points of his collar reached exactly the prescribed position above his chin, and his hair was arranged in the wind-swept style set by the Prince Regent.

His Hessian boots owed their fine polish, if Nanette was to be believed, to champagne.

"Champagne!" Prunella wanted to cry out loud, when he had no money and was doubtless accumulating a pile of debts!

When he left, after paying more extravagant compliments to Prunella and holding Nanette's hand far longer than was necessary, there was no doubt that he had left an impression that was not easy to erase.

Nanette was starry-eyed the whole evening and Prunella knew that whatever she might say to disparage Pascoe Lowes, it would fall on deaf ears.

"What am I to do?" she asked herself when she went to bed that night, and it was a question she had been repeating over and over again all through the week.

She heard her bedroom door open and knew that it was Charity, the maid who had looked after her ever since she was a child, who was carefully crossing the room towards the window.

Charity, who had been inflicted with such a cruel name by the Orphanage in which she had been brought up, was getting on in years.

But because she had been well trained she still moved as silently as when she had come to the Manor first as an under under-housemaid, then as a Nurserymaid, and finally, soon after Nanette had been born, she had been promoted to Nanny.

Now she was lady's-maid, Housekeeper, and self-appointed Chaperone to Prunella and Nanette since Sir Roderick had died.

Prunella had toyed with the idea of having an elderly lady to live with them, but she did not know anyone suitable, and also she knew that it would be depressing and a restriction that she would find intolerable.

"We live very quietly," she told herself, "and anyway there is little more the County can say about us that has not been said already."

At this there was a hardness in her eyes and a bitter twist to her lips, before deliberately she turned her thoughts elsewhere, and that inevitably was to Nanette.

Charity pulled back the curtains and the sun-shine flooded in through the windows. Then she turned towards the bed, and Prunella knew before she spoke that she had something to relate.

"What is it, Charity?" she asked, instinctively feeling that it would not be good news.

"Another letter came for Miss Nanette this morning," Charity replied, "and it was almost as if she knew clairvoyantly it was a-coming. She was down the stairs and at the front door before Bates could get there!"

"Was she already dressed?" Prunella asked.

"In her dressing-gown she was! I says to her: 'Really, Miss Nanette, you ought to be ashamed of yourself, coming down the stairs in a way no lady would!' "

"What did she answer?" Prunella enquired.

"I might as well have been talking to the wall!" Charity replied. "She just rushes past me, hugging the letter to her chest, goes into her bed-room, and I hears the key turn in the lock."

Prunella sighed.

"Oh, Charity, what are we to do about her?"

"I haven't the least idea what we can do, Miss Prunella, and that's the truth!" Charity replied. "I don't know what your father would have said if he could have seen her, going to the front door in her bed-attire, with the men-servants about!"

It was obvious that Charity was extremely shocked by it and in fact so was Prunella.

Not that Bates really mattered, for he had

been with them almost as long as Charity had, and the only footman they had at the moment was Bates's grandson, who was rather simple and not likely to notice what anyone was wearing.

It was the principle of the thing that mattered, and Prunella told herself that it was her duty to rebuke Nanette and to make her promise it would not happen again.

Charity had gone to the bedroom door to bring in a tray on which were a pot of the finest China tea, a slice of very thin bread, and butter.

She set it down on the table beside Prunella, saying as she did so:

"Mrs. Goodwin brought surprising news this morning!"

Prunella, pouring her tea, waited without much interest to hear what it was.

Mrs. Goodwin was one of the women on the Estate who came in to help with the scrubbing, but she spent more time talking than she did keeping the passages clean.

"She says, Miss Prunella," Charity went on, "that Mr. Gerald came back last night!"

Prunella put down the tea-pot.

"Mr. Gerald?" she repeated with a questioning note in her voice.

"I suppose I should say 'His Lordship' but somehow it comes strangely to the tongue."

Prunella's eyes were suddenly very wide.

"You are not saying . . . you cannot mean . . ."

"Yes, Miss Prunella, the new Earl of Winslow's home, if Mrs. Goodwin's to be believed. And after fourteen years!"

"It cannot be true!" Prunella gasped. "I had begun to think he would never come back."

"Well, he's here now," Charity said, "and if you asks me, he's only come to see what he can sell!"

"Oh, no!"

Prunella only breathed the words, but they seemed to come from the very depths of her being.

As Charity moved across the room to the wardrobe, Prunella said, almost as if she spoke to herself:

"The Earl is a relative of Pascoe Lowes, and . . ."

Her voice trailed away, but Charity heard what she had said.

"If you're thinking he'll be any help in stopping that overdressed young gentleman from pursuing Miss Nanette, Miss, I think you're mistaken. He's as bad, if not worse, than his nephew!"

There was no need to elaborate, because Prunella had heard all her life of the indiscretions and the raffish behaviour of the Earl's only son, Gerald.

When he had been living at home, the Estate, the village, and the County had talked of nothing else but his escapades, his wild parties, his fashionable friends, and the beautiful, alluring women whom he pursued and, if rumour was to be believed, who pursued him.

17

Then in 1803 during the Armistice between France and England things came to a climax.

Prunella was only seven and at the time was quite unaware of what was going on, but the tale had been related to her so often all through her life that she knew it as well as she knew her Catechism.

By this time it had been varied and embellished until she would have found it hard, if she had been hearing it for the first time, to believe it could possibly be true.

Knowing the old Earl as well as she did, there was no doubt that he, like all autocrats, was determined to have his own way, and apparently his son was the same.

They were both obstinate, self-willed, and undoubtedly overbearing, and the Earl had told Gerald that his philanderings were to cease, that he was to stop spending so much money, and that the best thing he could do would be to marry and settle down.

But Gerald had replied that he had no intention of doing any such thing.

"Like two fighting cocks they was!" one of the old retainers had said to Prunella. "Neither of 'em would give in, and when His Lordship knew he was being defied he loses his temper!"

Prunella had seen the old Earl in a temper many times and knew it was an extremely awesome sight, but she had learnt that Mr. Gerald had a temper too.

They had therefore been evenly matched, but

the outcome had been that the old Earl had threatened to cut his son off without a penny and had loaded the threat with many insults.

Gerald had told his father exactly what he could do with his money.

"Fine words!" the old Earl had sneered. "But you will soon find yourself in 'Queer Street' without it and come running back to ask for my help!"

"I would rather die than do that!" Gerald had replied. "So you can keep your damned money, your advice, and your everlasting disapproval of everything I do. As for my inheritance and this Estate by which you set so much store, it can rot for all I care and the house can fall to the ground before I would raise a finger to stop it!"

He could not have said anything which would have infuriated the Earl more, but before he could think of a suitable reply Gerald had gone.

The next thing they learnt was that "young Mr. Gerald" had left England, taking with him the pretty young wife of one of their neighbours, and her elderly husband was threatening to "shoot him down like a dog"!

From that moment there had been silence.

A month later war had started again with France, and all that was known was that Gerald had left England, and if he had gone to Paris, as seemed likely, the lady who had left with him had not returned.

There were a few people who escaped from the prisons in which Napoleon had confined all the

British tourists, but Gerald was not amongst them.

It was five years before it was learnt quite casually that the lady who had left England with him had died of cholera in the East.

Whether or not Gerald had died with her was not known at the time, but Prunella remembered that four years ago the Earl had told her father that he had received a letter from a friend informing him that Gerald had been seen in India.

There was no question of his coming home, and it would have been difficult unless he travelled in a troop-ship, for although Britain "ruled the waves" it was a long passage from India and a dangerous one.

The only ships that made the six-month voyage were those taking soldiers out or bringing them home.

A year before Prunella's father died, the Earl of Winslow had a stroke.

He had got into one of his rages, and when he dropped unconscious to the floor, it was impossible to save him, and although he lingered for two or three months he finally died.

It was partly the loss of his old friend, Prunella thought, that had made her father relinquish his already frail hold upon life.

She had nursed him day and night because he disliked having strangers about him, and he clung to her in a manner which made it almost impossible for her to do anything else.

If she was not there in his bedroom in the day-time he called her, and even at night he would send for her two or three times for no reason except that he wanted to see her.

This did not prevent him from being queru-lous, irritable, and difficult as only an invalid can be, and when finally he died Prunella herself was exhausted to the point of collapse.

It was Charity who had put her to bed, and she had slept without waking for forty-eight hours.

"I must get up," she had said weakly when she realised that she had lost two days out of her life.

"You'll stay where you are, Miss Prunella!" Charity had said firmly.

"But . . ."

"Miss Nanette and I can cope. Go back to sleep, Miss Prunella, and I'll wake you when we needs you."

Because she felt so tired and so weak, Prunella had done as she was told.

She knew afterwards that Charity's treatment had really saved her from a breakdown from sheer fatigue.

At first she could hardly believe that she was free to live a life of her own without hearing her father call her, without finding herself thinking of his comfort every second of the day.

Then she found that there were a great many things to be done which only she could do.

Now as she got up and dressed, she found her-self wondering whether the new Earl would behave like his father.

Surely, after being away so long, he would want to make reparation for the past and take up his position as head of the family.

The old Earl had always looked and behaved rather like a Biblical character, and although Prunella could hardly remember his son, she felt sure that he would want to follow the long succession of Winslows who had lived at the Hall and made it a place of importance not only to the Winn family but in the surrounding countryside.

Then as she buttoned her gown she suddenly remembered, almost as if someone had struck her, what Charity had said.

"He's come back looking for money, I suppose."

The words seemed to echo and re-echo round her bedroom and she knew that the new Earl of Winslow was going to have a shock which would doubtless be a very unpleasant one.

Two hours later Prunella stepped into the old-fashioned but well-sprung carriage drawn by two well-bred horses and set off for the Hall.

The old coachman who was driving her was not surprised when she told him where she wished to go, and she wondered if he knew that the Earl had returned.

After all, news about him would run like wildfire through the Estate, and if Mrs. Goodwin knew, then so would everybody else by this time.

Prunella gave a little sigh.

It was not going to be an easy interview and

she wished somebody could have gone with her to give her support.

She knew that Nanette would be worse than useless, especially after this morning when she had received the letter from Pascoe, and besides, what she had to say to the Earl when she had explained everything else was something her sister must not overhear.

She could have taken Charity, but she could not help thinking with a little smile that her stringent comments on "Mr. Gerald's" past behaviour would not help the situation.

It was difficult to anticipate what his attitude would be.

The carriage carried Prunella through the village, with its black-and-white Inn on the other side of the Green, the small pond on which there were always a few ducks, and the old Alms Houses that had been built by the previous Earl in more prosperous days.

The horses turned in through the gates to the Hall with their stone lodges on either side. They were occupied by gate-keepers who by now were so old and decrepit that they were no longer capable of attending to the gates; which were therefore left open permanently.

There was a long drive which wanted gravelling, bordered by oak trees which needed attention, then there was the lake with its banks overgrown with irises, and beyond it was the Hall.

It was beautiful architecturally, in that it was

designed by Inigo Jones, but the bricks needed pointing and there were a number of panes missing from the top-floor windows.

Yet Prunella could see that the first and second floor were not only in good repair but shining because they had recently been cleaned.

The carriage stopped at the steps leading up to the front door, which she noticed was open.

Dawson, the coachman, was too old to get down to assist Prunella to alight, but she managed it herself and stepped out.

"Shall I wait here for ye, Miss Prunella," he asked, "or go round to the back?"

She hesitated a moment, then replied:

"I think you should go round to the back, Dawson, and find out what is happening, and if the Carters are all right. They may be upset by His Lordship's unexpected return."

"I'll do that, Miss Prunella."

She did not wait to say any more but hurried up the steps and walked in through the open door.

As she had expected, there was nobody in the main Hall, and although she was feeling a little nervous she walked resolutely towards the Library, which she felt was where the Earl would be.

But the Library was empty, and so was the large Salon where the shutters had not been opened and the furniture was still covered with Holland dust-sheets.

She thought for a moment, then walked up the

staircase, with its exquisite Seventeenth Century ironwork, towards the Picture-Gallery.

She had a feeling almost like a pain in her heart that she knew she would find the Earl there and why he was there.

She was not mistaken. In the Gallery which ran the whole length of the central block was a man.

He had his back to her and for a moment she did not notice that he was tall and very broad-shouldered, but she saw that he was staring at a picture which had been painted by Van Dyke.

Prunella's lips tightened. Then as she walked slowly down the Gallery he must have heard her footsteps, for he turned his head and she saw that Gerald, the sixth Earl of Winslow, did not look in the least what she had expected.

Somehow, because she had always heard so much about his wild, raffish behaviour, she had expected him to look dandified and perhaps to bear some resemblance to his nephew Pascoe.

The man who turned to watch her approach, with what she thought was an expression of surprise in his dark eyes, was so casually dressed that it told her more surely than anything else that Charity was right: he had come back to find something to sell.

His coat was cut on the right lines but was somewhat loose-fitting, there was nothing special about his pantaloons, and his boots definitely needed polishing.

As for his cravat, Prunella was sure that

Pascoe would view it with horror, and even to her eyes it looked loose and comfortable rather than elegant and restricting.

What was strange was that his skin was so brown, and it took Prunella a second to remember that he had been in India and was therefore sunburnt.

While she was scrutinising the Earl, he was doing the same to her. In fact, he was wondering who this woman could be and trying to recall if he had ever seen her before.

Then as she drew nearer he was aware that she was too young for him ever to have met her.

He had at first been deceived, by the plain grey of her gown and her bonnet trimmed with grey ribbons, into thinking she was perhaps middle-aged.

Then he saw that her oval face, which was dominated by two very large grey eyes, was that of a young woman and that she was looking at him critically and with, understandably, an expression of disapproval.

As she reached him he asked:

"May I enquire if you have called to see me, which seems unlikely? Or have you another reason for being here in the Hall?"

Prunella dropped him a little curtsey.

"I am Prunella Broughton, My Lord. My father, Sir Roderick, who unfortunately died a year ago, was a very close friend of your father."

"I remember Sir Roderick," the Earl replied, "and I fancy I can now recall a small, pretty child who used to accompany him when he came here, who undoubtedly was yourself."

"I am gratified that Your Lordship should remember me," Prunella answered, "for I have something to tell you which I think you should know."

"I shall of course be delighted to listen, Miss Broughton," the Earl answered. "As you are doubtless aware, I arrived here only last night, and I was just now reacquainting myself with my ancestors."

As he spoke he indicated a portrait for the second Earl, and despite her resolution to remain calm Prunella gave a little cry.

"Oh, please," she said, "if you are going to sell any of the paintings, do not sell that one. It is the very best of them all, and your father used to relate that when Van Dyke had finished it, he said to your forebear: 'I shall never do a better portrait and this actually is the moment I should die!' "

As her voice died away there was silence. Then the Earl said:

"You are implying that I am intending to sell some of these paintings?"

"I was afraid that was in your mind, My Lord," Prunella answered, "and if you will permit me to do so, I will show you a list I have made of things in the house which would fetch quite a considerable sum but which would not be so cruelly missed by the future generations as the paintings in this Gallery."

"I do not understand," the Earl said, and his voice was dry, "why you should concern yourself, Miss Broughton, so closely with my private affairs."

Prunella drew in her breath.

"That is what I have come to . . . explain to Your Lordship."

The Earl looked round as if he was going to suggest that they sit down, but the chairs in the Gallery were all covered to prevent them from fading, and as if it was obviously what was in his thoughts, Prunella said:

"It would be best, I think, if we went down to the Library. I have always kept that room open."

"*You* have kept it open?" the Earl questioned.

He saw a faint flush come into her cheeks as she said:

"That is another thing I am going to . . . explain to you."

"And I shall be very interested to hear your explanation," he replied.

She thought there was an edge to his voice, as if already he resented her.

They walked in silence back along the Gallery, down the staircase, and into the Hall.

When they reached it a man appeared who Prunella guessed was a valet.

"So there y'are, M'Lord!" he said in what she privately thought was a slightly familiar tone. "I was thinking, as there's nothing to eat in the house I'd best pop down to the village and buy something."

"All right — do that," the Earl agreed.

The valet would have turned away but Prunella said quickly:

"I am afraid there is not much to buy in Little Stodbury, but if you go to the Home Farm you will find that Mrs. Gabriel will let you have an excellent ham that she has cured herself, and you could ask, when they are slaughtering their sheep, if they would keep a leg for His Lordship."

"Thank ye, Ma'am," the valet said.

"And of course, as Mrs. Carter should have told you, the Home Farm will provide eggs, milk, and butter, but I am afraid you will have to pay for them."

She looked a little anxiously at the Earl as she said:

"The arrangements they had with your father have lapsed since his death, and as they have to struggle to make two ends meet, they could not provide you with food for nothing."

"I did not intend to ask them to do so," the Earl replied sharply.

He turned to his valet.

"Pay for everything as you go, Jim."

"Very good, M'Lord."

As the valet disappeared Prunella could not help wondering where the money was coming from.

It seemed strange that the valet did not ask his master for any, and she thought it might be his own he was using until the Earl could sell something in the house and pay him back.

Once again she felt that pain within herself at the thought of parting with the treasures she had known and admired ever since she was a child.

At first, when they had been so isolated during the war, with the horses commandeered by the Army and with the younger men either away fighting under Wellington or enjoying themselves in the world of gaiety created by the Regent, the old Earl had been very lonely.

He used to encourage Prunella to borrow books from his Library because, he said, it was good for her education, but really it was because he liked talking to her and otherwise nobody except the servants came to the big house.

He would tell her tales about the paintings and the furniture, but because he was obsessed by the family and what it meant to him, his stories were nearly always about his ancestors, who had been soldiers, Statesmen, explorers, gamblers, and Rakes.

And now, she thought, another Rake had come home to diminish a treasure-chest which to her was part of history and which, because she too lived a very quiet life, was somehow part of herself.

They reached the Library and the Earl stood back for her to enter first.

She did not know why, but she felt he did it almost mockingly, and then as they walked into the room Prunella was suddenly acutely conscious of how shabby it looked.

She had never noticed it before, but now, as if she were seeing it with a newcomer's eyes, she realised that parts of the carpet were threadbare, the covers on the chairs had faded, and the linings of the curtains were in such rags that it was impossible for them to be mended any more.

She wondered if the Earl was thinking that things had been neglected since he had gone away.

She seated herself in an arm-chair at the side of the fireplace while he stood with his back to it, his hands deep in the pockets of his breeches, looking at her in an uncompromising manner.

"Well, what is all this about?"

Ever since she had arrived at the Hall Prunella had been holding in her hand a notebook, which she now placed on her lap as she said:

"I . . . I suppose it would be polite of me first to . . . welcome you home and say that . . . although your return is unexpected, it is . . . better late than never!"

"Do I detect a note of condemnation in your voice, Miss Broughton?" the Earl enquired.

"You must realise, My Lord, that since your father died things have been very . . . difficult."

"Why?"

"To begin with, no-one had any idea where you were, and secondly there was nobody to look after the Estate."

"What happened to Andrews? I always understood that he was a perfectly capable man."

"Fourteen years ago he was," Prunella an-

31

swered, "but, as it happens, Mr. Andrews has been bedridden for the last eighteen months, and for some years before that he was really incapable of getting round the Estate, even when somebody could drive him."

The Earl appeared to digest this information for a moment before he said, with a slight curl of his lips:

"Surely somebody has been engaged to take his place?"

"And how would he be paid?" Prunella enquired.

There was silence. Then the Earl asked:

"Are you telling me there is no money?"

"If I speak frankly and truthfully, My Lord, the answer is 'yes.' "

"But why? I understood — I always believed my father was a rich man."

"And so he was when you left home. But I think perhaps he had not as much capital as you thought, or else it was badly invested. Anyway, My Lord, many people's fortunes dwindled during the war, and Estates like this ceased to be profitable."

"Why? Why?" the Earl asked sharply.

"The tenants grew old and became incapable of farming their land properly, and they could not afford to employ enough men, even if they could have got them. Most able-bodied men were in the Army or the Navy, and gradually things deteriorated."

This news obviously shook the Earl, and she

saw by the expression on his face that it was something he had not expected, and it made him knit his brows and set his lips in a tight line. Then he asked:

"I am quite prepared to believe what you tell me, but I want to know how you come into this."

Prunella looked down at the book on her lap as if it gave her some comfort. Then she said:

"When my father was alive, he . . . helped yours in . . . one way or another."

"Are you telling me that my father borrowed money from yours?"

Prunella nodded her head.

"I would like to be informed of how much, and I expect, of course, to repay you."

"There is no need for that. It was not a loan but a gift."

"I shall look upon it as a debt!" the Earl said in an uncompromising voice.

Prunella did not speak, and as if he thought he had sounded rude he said quickly:

"But of course I am extremely grateful. I am only astonished that my father should have needed help of that sort."

"What worries me," Prunella said, "is what will . . . happen now."

"What do you mean by that?"

"There are certain pensioners who, if they are not paid, will starve because . . . they are old . . . past work . . . and there is nowhere else they can . . . go."

"Who has been paying these pensioners?"

There was silence until he said, even more sharply:

"I want to know the truth, Miss Broughton!"

"Since my father's death . . . I have," she replied.

She raised her eyes to his as she added:

"I was not interfering . . . it is just that they are people I have known all my life, and so the ones who were active worked here in the house for very little, but it kept them from starvation and I could not bear to see everything going to rack and ruin and covered in dust."

"So you paid *my* employees to keep *my* house in order?"

"It sounds a strange thing to do," Prunella said, "but because I came here so often when your . . . father was alive . . . and because I have always . . . known and loved the Hall, it meant almost as much to me as my . . . own house."

"And what else did you do?"

"I have put it all down in this little . . . notebook," Prunella replied. "Those who are receiving small pensions every week . . . so that they can keep alive . . . those who can work and earn a little money . . . although it often has to be supplemented . . . and the rents that are coming in more or less regularly."

She gave a quick glance at the Earl's face and was afraid of what she was seeing, before she added:

"In some cases . . . I cancelled the farmers' rents . . . altogether."

34

"Why did you do that?"

"You do not . . . understand," Prunella answered, and now her voice rose a little. "Since the war ended, the farmers have found that the prices for their produce have fallen disastrously. What is more, this year many of the County Banks have closed their doors and people have lost their savings of a lifetime."

The Earl did not speak and she went on:

"It is bad enough having thousands of men pouring out of the Army and the Navy without being given pensions, without any recompense for their injuries. The cost of living has gone up and for most of them there is no work. I had to take care of the people on this Estate . . . there was nobody else."

The Earl walked across to the window to stare out onto the lake and the Park beyond it.

"You must of course accept my gratitude, Miss Broughton," he said. "I am only surprised that you should have been so generous."

He did not sound very grateful and she felt that the way he praised her was not exactly a compliment, but she replied:

"If you are really grateful . . . then I want to ask you to do . . . something for me."

The Earl turned from the window and now there was a smile on his lips.

"So you are human after all!" he said. "I began to think you were some strange philanthropist who was doing good if not for your soul then perhaps for mine — and now, if you have a human frailty, I shall believe after all that you are real."

Prunella stared at him in sheer astonishment. Then she said sharply:

"I assure you I am real, My Lord, and the favour I have to . . . ask you is a very real trouble to me."

"I am waiting to hear it," the Earl said.

Now she felt, and she could not think why, that he was definitely mocking her.

Chapter Two

The Earl sat down in a chair on the other side of the hearth-rug.

He crossed his legs, sat back at his ease, and regarded her with what she thought was a slight smile on his lips.

Because she had felt slightly embarrassed ever since coming to call on the Earl, she had not looked at him very closely. Now she thought that his eyes in his suntanned face were definitely penetrating, although his eye-lids drooped a little lazily, as if he regarded life cynically.

There was something about his whole attitude that she resented.

She thought it was what she might have expected to feel about a man who, having left his home in such a reprehensible manner, had returned to be critical of everything that had been done in his absence.

There was a distinct silence before the Earl said, again with a mocking note in his voice:

"I am waiting, Miss Broughton, and of course, being deeply in your debt, I am prepared to be very sympathetic towards anything you require of me."

Prunella felt she wished to challenge this statement, but there was no excuse for doing so, and after a moment she said:

"What I am asking you to do, My Lord, is to prevent your nephew from paying attention to my sister."

The Earl raised his eye-brows and she knew this was something he had not been expecting.

"My nephew?" he asked.

"Pascoe Lowes, the eldest son of your sister, Lady Lowestoft."

The Earl smiled.

"I suppose I had forgotten his existence," he said, "because, as you may be aware, since I have been abroad my relations have not communicated with me. But it would interest me to know why my nephew should not pay his addresses, if that is what he intends to do, to your sister."

Prunella's back was stiff and her voice was hard as she replied:

"I will be frank with you, My Lord. Pascoe Lowes has a reputation, which I understand is fully justified, of being a fortune-hunter. He is also a Dandy."

Her tone was contemptuous and to her surprise the Earl laughed.

"He has certainly got on the wrong side of you, Miss Broughton. In fact, I feel quite sorry for him."

"There is no need for you to do that," Prunella said sharply. "But as my sister is only seventeen, she is young and impressionable."

"Then where did she meet my nephew?"

"In London. My father died a year ago and we were out of mourning in March. I therefore arranged for Nanette to be presented at Court."

"*You* arranged it?" the Earl remarked. "I see you lead a very busy life, Miss Broughton. You not only arrange my affairs but also those of your sister. Surely you have some assistance?"

"Since my father's death we have been living alone at the Manor," Prunella explained, "and as we live very quietly, there has been no need to have anybody living with us."

"You refer to your quiet life," the Earl said. "It surprises me. This used to be a lively place and there were many large houses with very hospitable owners."

He spoke almost as if he was reminiscing to himself, and therefore he was surprised when Prunella said in a repressed voice:

"I am sure, now that the war is over, that you, at any rate, will find quite a number of people ready to entertain you, My Lord."

As she spoke she thought that because he was the Earl of Winslow and unmarried, their neighbours would be too curious not to wish to meet him, even if he could not return their hospitality.

"So, while I can be entertained, you have not been so fortunate," the Earl remarked.

Prunella felt he was being uncomfortably perceptive and there was a distinct pause before she said:

"I have been in mourning for a year."

"And before that?"

"May I point out that my life is none of your business, My Lord?"

"That seems extraordinary!" the Earl remarked. "You have made my life your business. You have taken over control of my household and apparently my Estate, and yet now, because I am interested in you as a person, you are closing the door on me."

Prunella had the feeling that he was deliberately pursuing the subject simply because he was aware that she did not wish to talk about herself.

Then she said desperately:

"I wish to speak to Your Lordship about your nephew."

"That is what I understood. At the same time, I am trying to get a picture of what is happening, and unaccountably, Miss Broughton, you are refusing to assist me."

"What I was thinking," Prunella said quickly, "is that now that you are home, I am quite certain your nephew will ask you for financial help."

"Why do you imagine he will do that?" the Earl asked.

"For one thing, I presume he is your heir, and also . . ."

"And for another?"

She did not reply and the Earl said:

"It would be a mistake not to finish that sentence and keep anything from me."

"Very well," Prunella said. "I learnt yesterday that a week ago, when he was staying in the County, Mr. Lowes visited your father's Solicitors to find out if it would be possible to take steps to prove that you were dead, in which case he wished to put forward a claim for the house and its contents."

The Earl said nothing and Prunella went on:

"Surely you understand that would mean he would sell it. He would have no wish to live here, because he obviously prefers London, and anyway he could not afford to do so . . . and . . . and the Van Dykes would go first."

She spoke with a passionate note in her voice, and the Earl said, almost drawling the words:

"I can see that my paintings mean a great deal to you, Miss Broughton, but after all they are only paintings!"

"How can you say that when they have been handed down from father to son for two hundred years? When so many of them are of your ancestors and Inigo Jones designed the Gallery especially for them?"

"You are certainly very well informed, Miss Broughton."

He was being sarcastic but Prunella did not care.

"I consider them, as your father did, a sacred trust to be handed on to your children and their children, and not to be disposed of by any 'n'er-do-well' who wants money to throw away at the gaming-tables or on women!"

Her voice seemed to ring out and again the Earl laughed.

"Well done, Miss Broughton! And of course I

41

understand only too well what you are saying, having heard such tirades a thousand times, until I could stand them no longer and left England to prevent myself from having to do so again."

Prunella felt her spirits drop and the fire went out of her.

What was the point of talking?

Everything that had been said against him in the past must be true, and he was no better now than he had been when he ran away from his father, taking with him the wife of another man.

She thought that the best thing she could do was to leave with dignity and let the Earl, as he apparently wished to do, manage his own life in his own way.

Then she remembered how many people depended on her.

There were the old people in the two Lodges, who were so frail that in the winter she usually took them what food they required because they were incapable of walking even the short distance to the shop on the Green.

Then there were the farmers who could only just manage to produce the food they themselves needed and could not afford to do necessary repairs to their farm-houses, nor to the barns which had fallen down.

There were so many others. Even the Carters were long past retirement age, but there had been no cottage available, and they might just as well stay at the Hall and do what they could to keep it clean.

Her thoughts seemed to race through her mind, and all the time she was aware that the Earl was watching her, the mocking smile she disliked twisting his lips.

"Suppose we continue," he said after a moment. "You were telling me about my nephew and making it quite clear that you would not tolerate him as a brother-in-law."

"I will do anything to prevent it, My Lord!"

"Even come to me for assistance, although you are well aware it is asking the 'pot to call the kettle black'?"

Prunella thought this was only too true, and, as she could not think of a reply, she merely waited, her eyes on the Earl's face.

As if his thoughts were once again on her, he said:

"I assume, from what you have said, that your sister is an heiress, in which case I presume you are also one."

"No, My Lord."

"No?"

"My sister was left a considerable amount of money by . . ."

She hesitated before she ended:

". . . My mother."

"I believe I remember your mother," the Earl said reflectively. "Yes, I do remember her, and she was very beautiful. I am sorry to hear that she is dead."

Prunella did not reply, and when he looked at her he saw that she had dropped her eyes so that her lashes were dark against her cheeks and her lips were pressed together in what he thought was a hard line.

"I said I am sorry your mother is dead!"

"I heard you, My Lord."

"Where did she die?"

"I have no idea."

"You must be aware that you are making me curious?" the Earl remarked.

"I do not wish to speak of it, My Lord. I want to talk to you about Nanette."

"Nanette can wait," the Earl answered. "What is this mystery about your mother?"

Prunella rose from the chair in which she was sitting to walk to the window, even as he had done earlier in their conversation.

She stood looking out, and now that her figure was silhouetted against the light, the Earl could see that she was very slender and graceful, and it was only her grey gown, which he thought had nothing to commend it, that concealed the fact.

After a moment, as if she had made up her mind, she said, still with her back to him:

"I expect sooner or later you will be told what occurred, so it might as well be now."

The Earl was aware that she drew in a deep breath before she said:

"My mother . . . ran away . . . six years . . . ago!"

"It seems a somewhat prevalent exercise in

this part of the world," the Earl remarked.

"It is not something I can laugh about, My Lord, and now that I have told you, will you please not speak of it again? My mother's name was never mentioned in my father's house from the time she left."

There was silence. Then with a very obvious effort Prunella walked back from the window to the chair in which she had been sitting.

"It is obvious that, like myself, your mother could stand things no longer," the Earl remarked. "Did you miss her?"

"I have no wish to talk about my mother, My Lord."

"But I am interested," he insisted. "Now that I remember how beautiful your mother was, I think I am right in saying that your father was very much older than she was. In fact, he was a contemporary of my father, who was getting on for fifty when I was born."

Prunella did not reply, and the Earl, with a distinct twinkle in his eyes, continued:

"So the beautiful Lady Broughton followed my example and left a deadly existence of respectability and psalm-singing for what is popularly termed 'a life of sin'!"

He saw Prunella shudder, and finished:

"The punishment for which, of course, is fire and brimstone, hell and damnation, which is, I can assure you, far more pleasant and on the whole more enjoyable than what we left behind."

"I do not have to listen to this, My Lord."

"But you will do so because I want you to," the Earl replied. "I can see all too clearly, Miss Broughton, that you are condemning your mother to damnation as you condemn me and my nephew. I would be interested to know by what right you sit in judgement upon us."

"I am not judging, My Lord," Prunella protested, "I am only asking you to understand the position in which you find yourself now that you have come home, and I am trying to explain why, after your father died, I tried to save those who were suffering through no fault of their own."

"Very commendable!" the Earl remarked, but it did not sound like a compliment.

"Your private life is no concern of mine."

"But you are shocked by what you think I have been doing," the Earl insisted, "just as you were shocked by your mother."

As if he goaded her into a reply, Prunella said:

"Of course I was shocked . . . shocked, horrified, and disgusted! How could any woman leave her husband and her . . . family?"

"Her family!" the Earl replied softly. "That is the operative word, is it not? You minded her leaving you!"

For a fleeting second he saw the pain in Prunella's eyes as she looked at him, and he said in a different tone:

"When you are as old as I am, Miss Broughton, you will understand that for every

46

human action there are always extenuating circumstances, and if one has a kind heart and a perceptive mind, one can find them and understand."

Now it was her turn to be surprised, and her eyes were very large in her face as she looked at him before she said slowly:

"Perhaps you are . . . right. Perhaps I have not . . . looked further than what seemed to me to be a . . . wicked act of selfishness!"

"Did your mother leave alone?"

Again Prunella shuddered, and he felt as if it vibrated through her and came from the very depths of her being as she said, her voice barely above a whisper:

"N-no!"

"Then I imagine she was in love," the Earl said, "and love, my dear Miss Broughton, is something that is irresistible at the time, even if one is disappointed later."

The way he spoke made Prunella remember that he had been in love with the woman he had taken away with him when he had left.

She remembered the story had been that she was very pretty and they had met at first clandestinely while out riding, before finally they had disappeared together, leaving everybody shocked and horrified by their outrageous behaviour.

It was, Prunella thought now, not only a hatred for his father that had made Gerald storm out of the Hall swearing he would not return, but also that he had heard the irresistible call of love for a woman who was perhaps as unhappy in her environment as he was in his.

Then she realised that this was what had happened to her mother.

Of course it was true that she was very much younger than the man she had married straight from the School-Room.

Prunella's father had loved her in his own way, but she supposed that none of them had realised how unhappy and frustrated her mother had been before she had met . . .

Prunella stopped her thoughts.

She had sworn never again to think of the man she had utterly condemned for seducing her mother and taking her from them.

Because he had always been so charming to her she had, in an adolescent way, been in love with him herself.

She had thought he looked exactly as a gentleman should look. She admired the way he rode, and because he paid her the first compliments she had ever received she had cherished them and had taken more trouble over her appearance whenever she knew he was coming to the house.

That he should have betrayed not only her father but herself, by running away with her mother, had seemed a final act of treachery.

It had been so horrible, so unforgivable, that Prunella had told herself she loathed not only him but also her mother with a violence that made her feel murderous towards them.

"It was Mama who killed Papa!" she had said when her father died.

But she knew he had been ailing long before her mother had left, although perhaps it was because his wife had gone that he made no effort to get well or keep himself alive.

She had known when her father had clung to her that he was in a way making her a substitute for the wife who had deserted him.

Because she wanted to erase her mother's crime from his mind, her devotion to him had astonished everybody including the Doctors.

Yet she had known that deep in her heart it was not only love for her father but hatred for her mother which activated her.

Now the Earl, whose own life had been so reprehensible, was asking her to forgive, or rather, far more difficult, to understand her mother's motives and his own.

Because she felt at the moment as if he had created a chaos in her mind and she could not think clearly, she said:

"I would like, My Lord, to talk of your nephew. You said you would listen sympathetically to my request, and I am deeply perturbed by his pursuit of Nanette."

"I am prepared to talk about Pascoe," the Earl said, "but I want to get one thing quite clear: your mother left her money — and I am assuming she had a considerable fortune — to your sister and nothing to you?"

"I cannot see how that is of any importance to you, My Lord," Prunella replied, "but as it happens she divided it equally between us, and we were to have it when we became twenty-one."

She paused and the Earl interposed by saying:

"So when you reached that age you gave your share to your sister?"

"Yes."

"But you still have enough money of your own to spend on my Estate and my servants?"

"I have enough, My Lord, but Nanette is only seventeen and a fortune at that age is not only a responsibility but can also be a liability."

"You mean when a young man like my nephew is interested in her?"

"Exactly, My Lord!"

"I presume the money is in trust?"

"The Trustees are my father, who is dead, and the Solicitors who are also the Solicitors for your Estate. But the moment Nanette marries, the money of course will legally be administered by her husband."

"And she would wish that man to be my nephew?"

"I have already told you," Prunella said, a little edge to her voice, "that she is very young and very inexperienced. Your nephew is considered extremely handsome, and he behaves in an exaggerated manner, sending a Post-Chaise here from London with flowers and letters and paying her compliments which in my opinion are too glib and too suave to be sincere."

"And of course you are an authority on how a man would behave when he is in love?"

The Earl was mocking her again and Prunella told herself that she hated him.

Yet, because there was so much more at stake than her personal feelings for the Earl, she said:

"Please, My Lord, look at this sensibly and help me if you can."

"I think it is far more important that I look at it from your sister's point of view," the Earl said. "What I am going to suggest, Miss Broughton, is that I should have the privilege of calling on you in the near future, to meet your sister and to discuss not only her problems but my own."

He held out his hand and asked:

"Will you give me your notebook in which you say you have written everything that concerns my Estate? I will go into it at my leisure and see if I can understand what you have transcribed, although I daresay I shall need some explanations later."

Prunella could have handed him the book across the hearth-rug, but instead she rose to her feet and walked to his side.

He did not rise but took the book from her, opening it and seeing that she had set down in her neat, upright handwriting the names of all the pensioners, where they lived, their ages, and in what capacities they had been employed before being retired.

There were also the amounts of money they

had received and the dates on which it had been paid to them.

As she turned over the pages without speaking, Prunella said:

"I am afraid it will amount to rather . . . a lot, My Lord. That is why I have made out a list of the things that can be . . . sold."

"Yet you regret that they must leave the Hall?"

"Yes, of course, but I realise that the house needs a great many repairs done to it, and that too will be expensive."

"I thought that what I have seen so far seems in surprisingly good condition."

"We had to have a great number of the windows repaired after the winter gales," Prunella replied, "and one of the ceilings on the second floor fell down last month."

"I wish to have an account of the things you paid for, Miss Broughton."

"Yes, of course, but what is more important is that the pensions should continue."

The Earl was staring down at the notebook and Prunella said a little hesitatingly:

"Most of these will be . . . due next week . . . and I thought if you . . . could not find the money so . . . quickly, I could . . . lend it to you."

The Earl glanced up at her and she did not dare to look at the expression on his face.

"I can see, Miss Broughton, that you are quite certain I cannot manage my own affairs," he said.

She did not reply and after a moment he went on:

"As you quite obviously disapprove of me — I can feel it vibrating from you — I wonder that you do not leave me to go to hell in my own way."

Again Prunella felt he was peering at her, and almost despite herself she retorted:

"I am not preventing you from going to hell, My Lord, or anywhere else you fancy, but I cannot stand by and see you taking a lot of innocent people with you!"

The Earl shut the notebook with a slap.

"I must say," he remarked, rising to his feet, "that when I returned home last night I did not expect to find myself facing the Day of Judgement! It is almost, Miss Broughton, as if my father is still here, still determined that nothing I do is right."

Prunella sighed.

"I do not mean to make you feel like that, My Lord. But I was afraid that if you ever did return home you would misunderstand my motives in doing what seemed to me best."

"So you expected me?"

"Your father heard five years ago that you were alive and had been seen in India."

"And what was his reaction?"

"I think, although I cannot be sure," Prunella answered, "that he was glad. He was very lonely in the last years of the war, when my father was too ill to visit him and no-one ever seemed to come to the Hall."

"What you are saying is that there would have been a welcome even for me!"

"I think that is true, and I think he would have liked to make up your quarrel before he died."

She paused for a moment, then said:

"When I used to come here to see him, we often walked round the house together, and he would talk about you when you were very young. We even went up to the Nursery once and looked at your toys."

"I suppose you are telling me to make me feel contrite and ashamed."

Prunella did not answer, and after a moment he said:

"Perhaps if there had not been a war I would have come home earlier — I am not sure. But, as it was, the journey was almost impossible unless I had been a soldier."

"I can understand that."

"Well, there is nothing I can do about it now," the Earl said, "except to read your notebook, Miss Broughton, and of course to thank you for all you have done."

"I am not looking for your gratitude, My Lord. What I did was for your father and in a way for my own satisfaction. I love the Hall and I love all the people on the Estate, most of whom I have known ever since I was a child."

"How old are you?" the Earl asked unexpectedly.

"I am nearly twenty-two years of age."

"And yet you talk as if you had dedicated your life to the service of other people," the Earl said. "Why did you not go to London as your sister did, and why, which is more important, are you not married?"

"Quite simply, because I have not had the opportunity, My Lord."

"I am expected to believe that?" the Earl asked.

"It happens to be the truth. You see . . ."

She stopped, telling herself that it was none of his business what she did or did not do.

"I suppose," the Earl said, "what you are preventing yourself from telling me is that as your mother created such a scandal you have suffered for it."

It was the truth, but Prunella was angry with him for having guessed it.

"I had my father to look after for the last three years," she replied evasively. "He was very ill."

"You would not have been so important to him if your mother had been there," the Earl remarked.

"I have been perfectly content."

"That is untrue — and you know it!"

"I am not interested in myself but in Nanette, My Lord. I am finding it very difficult to make you keep to the point, which is that I have asked you a favour, and I beg you to concentrate on that and on nothing else."

"When I see your sister Nanette," the Earl replied, "I shall doubtless find myself involved in her problems whether I like it or not. For the moment, Miss Broughton, I am interested in yours, which seem to me to be very urgent."

"Urgent?" Prunella asked almost despite herself. "I do not . . . quite understand what you are saying."

"That is obvious," he replied. "We must find you a husband before your philanthropy gains such a hold that you are more interested in your soul than in your heart."

Three days later, Charity, when she called Prunella in the morning, had obviously some news to impart.

Although she was feeling somewhat heavy-eyed, Prunella forced herself to listen.

"Mrs. Goodwin says," Charity announced, "that there's ever so much activity going on up at the Hall and there's pictures being taken off the walls and stacked on the floors."

Prunella sat bolt upright in bed.

"From the Gallery? Oh, Charity, not from the Gallery?"

"Mrs. Goodwin didn't say where," Charity replied, "but there's more pictures in the Gallery than anywhere else."

"Yes, I know," Prunella sighed, "but I did ask him not to sell those."

She spoke the words almost beneath her breath, but Charity was not listening.

"Mrs. Goodwin also said as His Lordship sent for people from London and some of them arrived yesterday to see him. Tradesmen, they was, of some sort."

"Picture-Dealers!" Prunella murmured beneath her breath.

She had hoped that the Earl would come to see her yesterday, being sure that he would not do so the day after her visit. But although she had waited expectantly there had been no sign of him and now she knew the reason why.

Despite all she had said to him, despite the fact that she had left the list of what she thought could be sold without damage to the collection, he was selling the Van Dykes.

Of course they were likely to fetch more money than anything else, but how could he be so insensitive and part with them after all she had told him?

She was worrying too about the pensioners and the tenant-farmers.

Suppose he insisted on rent from the Jacksons? They would not be able to afford it and they would have to go. But Mrs. Jackson had been so ill during the winter and two of her children were always ailing.

"Why does he not come to see me?" Prunella asked herself not once but a dozen times.

Yesterday afternoon it had been extremely hard not to order the carriage and drive to the Hall to see for herself what was going on.

"I am sure Pascoe will want to visit his uncle," Nanette had said yesterday afternoon.

"Why should he know that he is here?"

Prunella asked stiffly.

"Because I wrote and told him the very first day he arrived," Nanette answered.

"Well, if Mr. Lowes has expectations in that direction, he is going to be disappointed," Prunella said sharply.

"You never think of anything but money, Prunella," Nanette complained. "Poor Pascoe cannot help it if his father's Estate is impoverished, just like that of the Winslows."

"I agree he cannot help it personally," Prunella replied, "but he need not be so extravagant. You should tell him, Nanette, that he is not to send you flowers and letters by Post-Chaise."

"Of course I could not do that," Nanette replied. "I think it is very kind of him and very, very romantic."

She gave a deep sigh.

"Oh, Prunella, I am so bored with being here and having nothing to do except wait for Pascoe's letters. Do you think you could write and ask Godmama if she would have me to stay with her just for a few days?"

"It would be useless for me to do so, and you only wish to go to London so that you can see Mr. Lowes. Your Godmother has already told me that she disapproves of the manner in which he is pursuing you, and she has made it quite clear, Nanette, as I have, that she thinks he is after your fortune and really has no interest in you apart from that."

"That is not true!" Nanette replied. "In fact it

is a lie, and I believe Pascoe when he says he would love me had I not a penny in the world!"

"He might love you," Prunella said, "but if he did, he certainly would not propose that he should marry you."

"How do you know? How can you be so unkind, so cruel about him?"

As she spoke Nanette jumped up from the chair in which she was sitting, and there were tears in her eyes.

She walked quickly to the door and only when she had reached it did she say:

"The trouble is, Prunella, that no man has ever looked at you, so you know nothing about love. When you die an old maid you will be sorry, very sorry for what you have missed!"

As she finished speaking Nanette went from the Drawing-Room, slamming the door behind her.

Prunella sat thinking miserably that she had made a mistake in saying what she had and wishing that she had been more tactful. But it had been difficult not to express her feelings.

Nanette had been walking about looking bored and unhappy except when she received letters from London, and, because there were no distractions locally, Prunella was racking her brains as to how she could turn her sister's yearning for Pascoe Lowes in another direction.

She remembered reading that the only antidote for one love-affair was another one, but how could she find a young man who would interest Nanette when they were isolated here at the Manor?

They were never invited to anything more exciting than tea at the Vicarage or to take part in the village Bazaar.

The Earl had been right in guessing that because of the scandal caused by her mother when she had run away, her daughters had suffered.

But it was only this year that the whole consequence of this had been revealed to Nanette.

While she was in the School-Room she not only had a Governess but teachers had come from the nearest towns to instruct her, because Sir Roderick believed that his daughters should have a good education and was quite prepared to pay for it.

When their father died, Prunella, knowing that the years of mourning would be a gloomy period, had sent Nanette to a fashionable Seminary at Cheltenham.

Therefore, it was only when she had returned from London that Nanette had found the quietness of the Manor and the fact that they never saw anyone but themselves almost insufferable.

Prunella had grown used to it, although sometimes she missed her father's voice calling her from his sickbed and the bustle of the Doctors arriving and leaving.

There had been medicines and luxuries to be fetched by the grooms and hundreds of other things which were required in the sick-room, which always resulted in the household being kept on its toes.

Now there was just the monotony of one day being exactly like another, except, of course, for the Earl's arrival at the Hall.

He had not called yesterday and Prunella felt that if he was busy selling his paintings, and doubtless also the tapestries and the silver, he would have no time left in which to be social.

She went downstairs to find her sister in the Breakfast-Room.

Nanette looked at her a little uncertainly, then, because she had a warm, impulsive nature, she ran to Prunella and flung her arms round her.

"Forgive me! Forgive me, dearest!" she cried. "I am sorry I was such a beast last night!"

Prunella put her cheek against Nanette's.

"Of course I forgive you," she said, "and really there is nothing to forgive. We have always understood each other, you and I."

"Until now."

She kissed Prunella again before she said:

"Dearest Prunella, you must try to help me. I cannot help being in love with Pascoe, and every day without him seems to pass like a century of time."

"It is only because you have not enough to do," Prunella said. "I have been thinking that perhaps I should write to our cousins who live in Bath. You might find it amusing to go there for a holiday, and I believe they have an excellent Theatre."

"I want to go to London!" Nanette said with a petulant note in her voice.

"I do not think we can possibly ask your God-mother to have you again so soon," Prunella said. "Surely you made some other friends when you were there?"

She was determined that Nanette should not go to London, knowing that she would do anything to see Pascoe Lowes. But she thought it would be diplomatic to pretend to agree and in that manner play for time.

Anyway, it might stop Nanette from moping, Prunella thought.

"I cannot think of anyone, but I will try," Nanette answered. "Most of Godmama's friends were either very smart and obviously did not wish to be bothered with a débutante, or else they had girls of their own and regarded me as a potential rival."

She thought Prunella looked surprised, and she laughed.

"Do not be so foolish, dearest Prunella! I am beautiful — at least Pascoe thinks so — and I am rich! The other girls had very little chance when I was round."

"What about the other gentlemen you met?" Prunella asked. "Your Godmother said there were two who would have proposed to you if you had given them any encouragement."

Nanette laughed scornfully.

"You should have seen them! One was a Baronet, old and rather fat, and the other was a

Marquis, but the girls called him 'the Chinless Wonder' behind his back, because he was so stupid. How could I have a husband like either of them?"

"No, of course not," Prunella agreed.

"When I marry," Nanette said in a soft little voice, "I want to be in love, and I *am* in love!"

The conversation always came back to the same point, Prunella thought as she helped herself to bacon and eggs.

She was determined not to antagonise Nanette as she had done last night, so she listened to her sister eulogising over the looks, cleverness, and charm of Pascoe Lowes, and wondered what she could do about it.

When breakfast was finished Prunella said:

"I was thinking that we might go riding this morning. I notice you did not exercise your horse yesterday, and you know it is bad for them not to be taken out regularly."

"All right, we will go riding," Nanette agreed without much enthusiasm.

Then as an idea struck her she asked:

"Could we not go in the Park?"

She was, of course, referring to the Park belonging to Winslow Hall, where they had always ridden in the past because it was so much bigger than their own and also because there was a long, flat stretch in one part of it that was a perfect place for a gallop.

The present Earl's grandfather had trained his racehorses there, and Prunella enjoyed the exhil-

63

aration of galloping when she knew there was no need to watch the ground for rabbit-holes or to be apprehensive about not being able to pull in her mount at the end of it.

She made up her mind.

"We will go to the gallop," she said.

If the Earl was busy selling his possessions he would not know what was happening in another part of the Estate, and, what was more, he would not be interested.

It was so painful to think of what he was doing that Prunella thought anything would be better than to sit at home, as she had done yesterday, expecting him, only to realise late in the afternoon that she had waited in vain.

Half-an-hour later, having changed into their riding-habits, the two girls set off on the horses which had always been their own.

"Pascoe says I should buy myself some horses at Tattersall's," Nanette confided conversationally as they rode down the drive, "and I think Dragonfly is getting too old and too staid for what I require."

Prunella knew it was only another excuse to go to London, so she said nothing.

Dragonfly was an excellent horse in every way and had cost a considerable sum of money when she had told their Head Groom to buy him eighteen months ago.

"Pascoe is very knowledgeable about horses," Nanette went on. "He wants to become a Corinthian, but I think he already drives better than anyone I have ever seen."

"You went driving with him when you were in London?" Prunella asked. "I hope you were chaperoned."

Nanette laughed.

"There is only room for two people in a Phaeton, and I cannot see Godmama perched up behind on the rear seat! All the girls were allowed to go driving in Hyde Park, but Pascoe's Phaeton was the smartest there! I could see everybody envying me when I drove with him."

There was nothing Prunella could do but listen, and she was glad when they rode across the top of Winslow Park towards the gallop.

When they reached it, there was no need to touch their horses with the whip, for they had been there far too often before not to know what was expected of them.

It was a wild, exciting gallop and Prunella felt as if it swept away some of her apprehension and the heaviness which had been with her when she had awakened because she was so worried.

She knew that Nanette was trying to beat her and she pressed her own horse, but eventually as they reached the end of the gallop they did so side by side.

Then as they drew in their horses, both laughing a little at the speed at which they had travelled, a man on horseback appeared through the trees and rode towards them.

It was the Earl, and Prunella looked at him, thinking he was riding exceedingly well.

Then she saw that he was astride a large black stallion which she had never seen before, and she knew it had certainly not come from the empty stables at the Hall.

Chapter Three

The Earl rode up to them and took off his hat.

"Good-morning, Miss Broughton," he said, then looked at Nanette.

Before Prunella could introduce her sister, Nanette exclaimed:

"You must be the new Earl! I have been so looking forward to meeting you!"

"I am flattered!" the Earl replied. "And I have heard a lot about you, Miss Nanette!"

Nanette gave him a mischievous glance as she said:

"None of it, I am sure, to my advantage!"

The Earl laughed.

"I hope, My Lord," Prunella said, "you do not mind us using the gallop?"

"As a matter of fact," Nanette said irrepressibly, before the Earl could speak, "we thought you would be too busy to know that we were here."

"I always used the gallop when I was a boy," the Earl said, "and I thought it would do Caesar good to exercise his legs."

"If that is Caesar," Nanette exclaimed, "I think he is the finest horse I have ever seen!"

"That is what I thought when I first saw him," the Earl replied.

Because it was difficult to restrain her curiosity, Prunella enquired:

"Where did you find him? I can hardly believe you brought him with you from India!"

"Jim must have the credit for discovering him," the Earl replied. "When we arrived at Southampton he heard there was a Horse-Fair in the vicinity and insisted on seeing if there was anything for sale that would enable us to arrive at the Hall quicker than if we came by carriage."

"And he found Caesar," Prunella remarked.

She thought it was strange that a valet should be a good judge of a horse, especially one as superlative as the stallion which the Earl was riding.

"Jim is very knowledgeable where horses are concerned," the Earl explained, "and he is anxious to fill the stables, which I find most depressingly bare."

With difficulty Prunella stopped the words that rose to her lips.

She could understand only too well what was happening.

The Earl had sold some of the paintings, and instead of spending the money on repairs that were necessary to the house, on the farms, and on the pensioners, he had chosen to spend it on horses and doubtless on women.

In her mind the two went together.

She thought of all the stories she had heard of the horses and carriages that the Bucks bought for enormous sums to give to the "Cyprians" and other ladies of easy virtue who took their fancy.

It had always shocked her that women who were what Charity described as being "no better than they should be!" should have so much money spent on them, when there were children starving in the slums and men who had served their country during the war now begging by the roadside.

As if her disapproval vibrated from her and the Earl was aware of it, he looked at her and after a moment he said:

"You apparently do not think Jim's idea, and of course mine, is to be commended, Miss Broughton."

"Your ideas on horse-flesh are not my concern, My Lord," Prunella replied.

"I think it is a wonderful idea!" Nanette exclaimed. "And I cannot think why Prunella should disparage it. After all, she loves horses."

"I can see that from the very fine, well-bred animals you are both riding," the Earl replied.

"I was just saying that I want to go to Tattersall's to buy myself a new horse," Nanette chattered on. "Dragonfly is too slow and not half as spirited as I can see Caesar is."

"I think you would find Caesar too much for you," the Earl replied, "but of course when there are more horses in my stables I should be delighted for you to ride them, Miss Nanette."

Nanette gave a cry of joy.

"Thank you, thank you, and do please hurry

and buy lots of horses so that I can avail myself of your kindness!"

"You will have to come and speak to Jim," the Earl said, "and I hope too that you will visit me."

Nanette gave a little laugh.

"You must be aware that I am longing to do so. I am so curious about you, and Prunella and I were both so disappointed when you did not call on us yesterday."

"You were expecting me?" the Earl enquired.

He looked at Prunella as he spoke, but she deliberately turned her head away so that he could not see her face.

"Prunella thought you would want to see her about a lot of things concerning the Estate," Nanette said. "After all, she has been fussing over it like an anxious hen ever since your father died, and she spends all her money on repairing your house and feeding your pensioners, so you ought to be very grateful to her."

Prunella's fingers tightened on the reins.

She was intensely embarrassed by what her sister was saying. At the same time, she did not know how to stop her.

While Nanette was talking she had turned her horse and now she and the Earl were both riding beside Prunella.

"I am of course extremely grateful," the Earl said, "and it is very remiss of me not to have called on you yesterday as I intended, but unfortunately I was detained by some people who arrived from London to see me."

'Picture-Dealers . . . silversmiths . . . and sharks,' Prunella thought to herself, but she forced herself to say nothing aloud, and Nanette went on:

"You must find it fascinating to come back, after being away for so long, to find everything just as you left it."

"Not quite," the Earl said. "The gardens are overgrown and the peach- and grape-houses are almost falling down."

Prunella stiffened, and, as if he was aware of the anger she was feeling, her horse fidgeted a little.

'How dare he!' Prunella thought to herself. 'How dare he complain? The gardens overgrown indeed! If I had not paid poor old Ives, he and his family would have starved to death, and as for the peaches and grapes . . . !'

If she had been speaking, words would have failed her.

As it was, only by keeping her lips tightly closed did she prevent herself from telling the Earl exactly what she thought of him.

"What I have been wondering," he was saying, "is if, in order to make up for my impoliteness, I could invite you and your sister to dine with me tomorrow evening!"

"We would love to!" Nanette said. "Would we not, Prunella?"

"I am not . . . sure we can manage it," Prunella answered in a cold voice.

"But of course we can!" Nanette insisted.

71

"You well know we have no other engagement, and it is years and years since I had a meal at the Hall. It would be great fun to be back there again with you."

She gave the Earl a flirtatious little look which she had learnt in London was very effective where older men were concerned.

"Then I shall look forward very much to entertaining you, Miss Nanette," he said, "and I feel that as we have known each other's families for so long — and unless I am mistaken we were introduced when you were in your cradle — I should be allowed to call you Nanette."

"But of course!" Nanette agreed. "And I would like to say that you are much, much nicer than I thought you would be."

"Thank you," the Earl said with a smile.

Because she could listen no longer to this exchange of pleasantries, Prunella touched her horse with her heel, and as he trotted ahead, Nanette turned towards the Earl.

"I want to talk to you," she said in a low voice.

"About my nephew?" the Earl enquired.

"Yes," Nanette said. "How did you guess?"

Before he could reply, she added:

"I suppose Prunella told you and has put you against him — a most sneaky, underhanded thing to do!"

"Let me say, before you work yourself up unnecessarily against your sister," the Earl said, "that I always rely on my own judgement where people are concerned."

"I know you will like Pascoe."

She smiled at him and he thought that Prunella had been right when she had said how lovely she was.

With her fair hair, blue eyes, and pink-and-white complexion, she was exactly the type of English girl that embodied the dreams of every young man when he was abroad and far away from home.

The Earl also appreciated the picture she made in her leaf-green riding-habit and her high-crowned hat encircled by a gauze veil.

Because Nanette did not wish her sister to know she had spoken to the Earl about Pascoe, she trotted after her, and as she did so the Earl turned and rode back through the trees in the direction of the Hall.

"It will be exciting to dine with him!" Nanette said as she caught up with Prunella. "I cannot think why you had to be so snooty about it."

"He will only be spending money he can ill afford."

"Oh, good heavens, Prunella!" Nanette exclaimed. "You cannot begrudge him a little amusement when he has been away for so long. Anyway, I want to see him again and talk to him."

"About his nephew?"

"Why not?" Nanette asked defiantly. "If he is as poverty-stricken as Pascoe, he might be sympathetic and all the more grateful to us."

"That is not the sort of thing you should say,"

Prunella said quickly.

"Why not?" Nanette asked again. "The Earl should be down on his knees thanking you for all you have done for the Winslow Estate, and I would like Pascoe to be grateful to me. As far as I am concerned, he can spend every penny I possess, and I will enjoy watching him do so!"

"Nanette, you are not to say such things!" Prunella said crossly. "Any man who had a vestige of pride would be ashamed to live on his wife's money."

"Papa never complained because Mama was rich," Nanette said with unanswerable logic.

"Papa had a great deal of money of his own," Prunella replied.

"Not really enough for you to spend all you want on the Winslow Estate. I suppose you told the Earl how you had to buy a new range for his kitchen and repaint the large Salon after it was spoilt by flooding?"

"I prefer not to talk about it."

"Oh, well, if you like spending your money in such a boring way, who is going to stop you?" Nanette asked. "But I can tell you one thing, Prunella, you must wear something pretty if you are going to dine with the Earl."

"The gowns I have are quite good enough."

Nanette laughed.

"You must be crazy! I have been thinking ever since I came back from London how old-fashioned and out-of-date you look, but I did not like to say so for fear of hurting your feelings."

Prunella looked in a startled manner at her young sister, then as she would have hotly denied the accusation she knew it was the truth.

She had in fact hardly thought about her appearance since her father had been so ill, except that when he died she had bought herself several black gowns from the nearest town.

Then, after six months, when she was in half-mourning she had augmented them with two gowns in grey and one in mauve.

She realised that while they were the best the country dressmaker could supply, they certainly bore little resemblance to the copious collection of elegant gowns which Nanette had brought back with her from London.

It was true, Prunella realised now, that with the end of the war fashions had changed. The very straight, plain, Grecian-type gowns, which had been the vogue at the beginning of the century and which were said to have been modelled on those introduced by Napoleon's wife Josephine, had given way to a much more elaborate style.

Now the gowns widened out at the hem, and although the waist remained high, both the bodice and the skirt of the gowns were amply decorated with lace or embroidery, frills or fringes.

Nanette's gowns were far more feminine and very much more attractive than anything Prunella had seen before.

And she learnt that older women in the evening wore turbans trimmed with feathers and jewels, while their day-dresses were embellished with gold braid, buttons, and even epaulettes until they appeared almost as dashing as a Dragoon on parade.

"Perhaps I do look a little dowdy," Prunella admitted humbly. "When I have time we must go shopping and you can help me choose some clothes that are more up-to-date. But tomorrow evening I shall have the choice of a black gown or one in grey."

"Then I absolutely refuse to go with you!" Nanette said. "From all I have heard, the Earl has an eye for beautiful women. And I rather like his raffish air. I can almost imagine him as a pirate or a buccaneer of some sort."

"I certainly do not think of him like that!" Prunella snapped.

"Whatever he is, he is still a man," Nanette said, "and although you often forget it, Prunella, you are a woman!"

"We can solve this problem quite easily by not dining at the Hall," Prunella said, "and I will send a message this afternoon to say so."

"If you do that, I shall go alone," Nanette threatened. "I want to dine with the Earl, and you cannot be so silly and prudish as to try to stop me."

Prunella did not reply and Nanette said:

"I know exactly why you are being so disagreeable to him. It is because he ran away centuries ago with that pretty Lady 'What's-Her-Name?'

and you still hold it against him."

"I am surprised that you know about such things!" Prunella exclaimed.

"Know?" Nanette repeated. "When everyone has talked about the 'goings on of Master Gerald' ever since I can remember? There was not one woman but dozens of them!"

She gave a little laugh.

"I think that instead of being told fairy-stories when I was a child, I was told of the exploits of the young heir at the Hall, and quite frankly, until I met Pascoe I thought Master Gerald was the Prince Charming I sought in my dreams."

"Really, Nanette, I am sure that is not true!" Prunella protested.

"It is! So we are both going to dress up and look our best. And as we are nearly the same size, you are going to wear one of my gowns until we can buy you something decent of your own."

Prunella laughed as if she could not help herself.

"You are the débutante, Nanette, not I."

"At the moment you are making me feel like an elderly Chaperone trying to launch a 'Country Miss' into the *Beau Monde!*" Nanette teased. "And goodness knows if you will sink or swim!"

"I have never heard such an outrageous . . ." Prunella began, only to realise that, laughing at her own audacity, Nanette was already galloping away.

The only thing Prunella could do was to follow her.

That afternoon when Nanette was busy writing a letter which Prunella guessed was to Pascoe and had no idea how she could prevent her sister from sending it, she decided to visit an old woman who had been Nurse to the Earl when he was a child.

She had wanted to explain to him that Nanny Gray was one of the people whom it was most important for him to see, because she was not only very old but had been praying ever since he had gone away that he would come home.

She had intended to tell the Earl this if, as she had expected, he called the previous day.

But as she had had no chance to talk to him since that first visit to the Hall, she knew that she must go and visit Nanny Gray herself.

If she had heard that the Earl was home she would be in a fever of anxiety to see "her baby," as she always called him.

It took longer than usual to get to Nanny's cottage, situated as it was on the other side of the Earl's Estate, because Prunella deliberately told old Dawson not to drive through the Park.

She felt that as she and Nanette had been caught trespassing once today, she did not wish the Earl to feel they were taking advantage of what had happened in the past or of the Manor's proximity to the Hall.

Accordingly, the horses drove her along the dusty country lanes until they reached another small village, which was known as "Lower

Stodbury" to distinguish it from the villages which were known as "Little Stodbury" and "Greater Stodbury."

It consisted of only a dozen cottages, all occupied by those who either worked on or were pensioners of the Winslow Estate, an Inn, a Church, and a very small shop.

Outside the village were various houses belonging to those who were slightly better off, besides a larger one, now closed and in a dilapidated state, which was the Dower House of the Winslow family.

As the last two Countesses had died before their husbands there had been no particular use for it, and Prunella had often thought it was a pity it could not be redecorated and perhaps let to people who would be an asset to the neighborhood.

'It is the sort of idea,' she thought bitterly, 'that would be of no interest to the Earl, even if he had the money to spend on it.'

She sighed and continued in her mind:

'If he has sold the Van Dykes, he will doubtless go to London, and once there, like his nephew, he will find it easy to become a fortune-hunter.'

She was certain, as her thoughts continued, that there would be plenty of women ready to surrender everything they possessed to wear the coronet of a Countess at the Opening of Parliament.

When that happened, the Earl would have plenty of money to spend on restoring the Hall, but it would be too late to save the Van Dykes.

Her thoughts about the Earl made her for the moment forget her surrounds, and with a start Prunella realised that Dawson had brought the horses to a stop outside Nanny Gray's cottage.

It was a little way outside the village and had been chosen for Nanny by the last Earl when she retired because it was better built and had a larger garden than those of his other pensioners.

Nanny had at first been proud of her new home, even though she missed being at the Hall, and when Prunella went to see her she found everything spotless, and Nanny, although she was often lonely, apparently was quite content.

Then as Nanny had grown older it had become more difficult for her to walk even as far as the small shop, and Prunella found that the old woman dwelt almost entirely in the past, saying: "Master Gerald did this" and "Master Gerald did that."

There were tales about "my baby" from when he was born to the moment when, with tears in her eyes, she had seen him off to School.

Nanny had also found, after being waited on and catered for most of her life, that it was difficult to adjust herself to doing her own housekeeping and cooking her own food.

Prunella had travelled almost daily to the small cottage last winter because she knew it would be impossible for Nanny to cook food for herself, much less to go out and buy what she needed.

Now she alighted at the cottage gate and walked up the garden-path noting that while it was colorful with flowers there was also a profusion of weeds and nettles.

She knocked on the door but did not wait for a reply and walked in. She knew it would be difficult for Nanny to move out of her chair.

"Is that you, Miss Prunella?" Nanny asked in a quavering voice.

"Yes, Nanny. How are you today?"

Prunella put down on the kitchen-table the basket she was carrying. It contained a pie which only needed heating, a sponge pudding, a newly baked loaf, a large pat of butter, and a pot of home-made strawberry jam.

"Is it true, Miss Prunella? Really true that His Lordship's come back?"

"Yes, Nanny, and I am sure he will be coming to see you."

"My baby! My baby's home after all these years!" Nanny cried.

She was very old and frail and her eyesight was failing, but for the moment there was in her voice a youthful excitement that Prunella had not heard for years.

"You'll tell him I'm still here, Miss Prunella? You won't let him think I've passed on?"

"No, of course not, Nanny," Prunella replied.

"He'll have to come soon," Nanny said. "Last night I dreamt I was being took, and it was an omen. I well knows that I'll not live thro' another winter."

"Now, Nanny, you must not talk like that," Prunella said. "You know how much we would miss you."

"I don't mind dying if I can see my baby again," Nanny replied. "It's the thought of him that's kept me going all these years."

"His Lordship would certainly not wish you to die as soon as he comes home, now would he, Nanny?"

"Is he wed?"

"No."

"I'm not surprised. I never thought he'd get round to marrying that lady who went off with him."

"I believe she is dead," Prunella said in a cold voice.

"A good thing too, if you ask me," Nanny observed. "She'd no right leaving her husband and running away with a boy not old enough to know his own mind."

"I always thought he knew that only too well," Prunella observed tartly. "After all, no-one made him run away."

"That's as may be, Miss Prunella, but I think His Lordship was to blame, always finding fault with Master Gerald. If Her Ladyship had been alive she'd have understood him, and I've often said to him myself: 'Take no notice what His Lordship says.' But he was never one to take things lying down."

Prunella thought this was doubtless true. At the same time, what had been the point of making himself an exile, doubtless in very un-comfortable circumstances, when he might have stayed at home and looked after his Estate?

Nanny began to ramble on about the old days and Prunella found her thoughts slipping away to think of the Earl and the woman he had run off with.

She wondered what his life had been like when he was living on the other side of the world.

Suddenly the door opened behind her, which made her start, for she had not heard the sound of carriage-wheels. Then Nanny's cry of happi-ness made her realise who had come into the cot-tage.

"Master Gerald! My baby! Is it really you?"

"Yes, I am here, Nanny," the Earl replied.

He seemed very large and almost overpower-ing in the small kitchen, and he moved across it to bend and kiss his old Nurse on the cheek.

"I knew you'd come!" Nanny Gray was saying ecstatically. "I felt in my bones that you were alive, even when they said you were dead, and as I was just telling Miss Prunella, now that I've seen you I don't mind dying."

"Why should you be talking about dying, Nanny," the Earl asked, "when I have only just come home? I want to talk to you. I need your advice."

"You need me, Master Gerald? I suppose I should say 'M'Lord' now that your father's dead, God rest his soul."

"I shall answer to 'Master Gerald' as I have,"

the Earl said with a smile, "and of course I want your advice, Nanny. I expect Miss Prunella has been telling you how ignorant I am of what has been going on here while I have been away for so long."

As he spoke he gave Prunella a glance which she thought was deliberately provocative, and she rose to her feet.

"Now that His Lordship has arrived, Nanny, I will say good-bye."

She put out her hand but the old woman held on to it.

"Now you stay where you are, Miss Prunella," she said. "I want to talk to His Lordship about you and tell him all you've done for us when there was no-one else after the old Master died. There would have been many more in the Church-yard if it hadn't been for you."

"Oh, please, do not say such things," Prunella said quickly. "His Lordship does not want to hear them."

"They have to be said," Nanny contradicted, keeping a tight hold on Prunella's hand. "It's an Angel of Mercy you've been, bringing us old ones food in the winter and paying the Doctor when he wouldn't call without it. One day, you mark my words, you'll get your reward."

"I am sure that is a long time away," Prunella said. "But now, Nanny, I must go. Dawson does not like the horses being kept waiting."

"That is the oldest excuse in the world!" the Earl remarked drily. "But I would like a word with you, so perhaps the horses can contain themselves for a little while longer?"

Prunella wanted to reply that it was not the horses who were fidgety but herself.

But because she thought it would be uncomfortable to argue in front of Nanny, she managed to release her hand, and instead of sitting down again she walked to the small diamond-paned window to look out onto the road outside.

The Earl was sitting close to Nanny and she heard him say:

"What I want you to tell me, Nanny, is what you need done to your cottage. Those I have visited so far seem to require a lot of renovation."

"I'm all right, Master Gerald, Miss Prunella's seen to that. The roof leaks a little in the top room when it rains, but it's not the one I use, so it doesn't matter that much."

"Nevertheless, it should be seen to," the Earl said.

He drew a small notebook from the pocket of his coat and wrote in it. Then he said:

"I have brought your pension, and in the future it will be trebled, but this week there is a little more in the packet than usual."

"That's very kind of you, Master Gerald, very kind indeed," Nanny said, "but then you always were a generous one. You're like your dear mother, who, as I've often told you, was the 'giving' sort, and it came from her heart."

"That is what is important, is it not, Nanny?" the Earl said. "And it was you who taught me that to give a present with love counts a dozen times more than if it is given with disapproval and contempt."

Although she did not turn her head, Prunella was aware that he glanced in her direction, and she knew that what he was saying was directed at her personally.

"I *have* given with my heart," she wanted to say.

But she knew that in a way he was right. She loved the people she had helped, but she hated him for his indifference and because he had neglected them by remaining abroad when he should have been at home.

Her small chin went a little higher as she listened to the Earl saying good-bye in an affectionate tone to his old Nurse, and she told herself he was only putting on an act for her benefit.

'He is trying to show me that he is sympathetic and understanding,' she thought.

She told herself that however much money he gave away, it was only to placate his conscience, but to do so he had sold the treasures that should have been preserved for the generations which would come after him.

"I will come and see you again soon, Nanny," the Earl said, "and if there is anything you want particularly, send someone to the Hall to let me know."

"I'm happy that you're here," Nanny answered, "and it's like old times to think of you where you were born."

"I am enjoying being home," the Earl said simply.

Then when he would have left she held his hand in both of hers, saying:

"Before I do die, Master Gerald, what I'd like is to hold your son in my arms and know that he was like you — and what a bonny boy you were, too!"

"But first I have to find myself a wife," the Earl said with a note of amusement in his voice.

"That shouldn't be difficult," Nanny replied. "You always had a way with the ladies, and I don't suppose you've lost it now that you've got older!"

The Earl laughed.

"You still remember my reputation, Nanny!"

"Nobody round here's likely to forget it," Nanny retorted, and the Earl laughed again.

"Good-bye, Nanny," Prunella said.

The old woman replied, but Prunella was sure that once they had gone, it was only the Earl of whom she would be thinking.

The Earl followed Prunella onto the paving-stones which ran from the door to the gate.

"May I drive home with you?" he enquired.

"What about your horse?" Prunella enquired, looking to where Jim, astride another fine animal, was holding Caesar's reins.

"Jim can bring him along behind," the Earl said.

"Very well, My Lord."

She wondered what he had to say to her, and

when they were seated in the carriage and Dawson started to drive back the way they had come, the Earl said:

"I have heard your praises extolled everywhere I have been. I realise more every moment how deeply I am in your debt, and I do not mean only financially."

"Country people always exaggerate," Prunella said, "and I do not want your gratitude. I am only glad that you remembered Nanny Gray."

"Of course I remembered her," the Earl replied, "even without the entries in your little black book. It is very helpful, but there are a number of omissions."

"Omissions?" Prunella asked sharply.

"Nanny mentioned two of them this morning."

"Oh . . . that!"

"Yes, that," the Earl agreed, "and of course the Carters were very voluble about what you have done to the house! I am getting the uncomfortable feeling that it is more yours than mine."

"What you are saying only upsets me," Prunella said sharply. "I explained to you exactly why I did some repairs at the Hall, and there is really no point in going over and over it again. Have you seen the farmers?"

"Some of them," the Earl replied, "and I am appalled by the conditions on the farms."

"Please do not throw them out . . . not the Jacksons . . . at any rate. They really have tried . . . and I know it would cost a fortune to put their farms back into working order . . . but I do beg you to let them stay where they are."

The Earl turned sideways in the carriage-seat to look at Prunella.

"I wonder where you get your impression of me and what you fancy is likely to be my behaviour?" he asked.

"Must one pretend to be ignorant of the fact that you have returned with no money to find that your inheritance is impoverished?" Prunella asked sharply.

"You sound almost as if you are blaming me personally for that."

"Perhaps in a way I am," she said. "I cannot help feeling, although I may be wrong, that if you had been here, you might have been able to prevent everything from getting to its present state."

"My father did not want my help, as he always thought Andrews was completely competent. And even though he was a close friend of your father, I doubt if he ever confided in him."

"I am quite certain he would have done nothing of the sort. When your father was ill everything went from bad to worse, and when he died it was the Solicitors who told me there was no money. So I did what I could, but you should have been here yourself."

"You speak very frankly, Prunella," the Earl remarked in a dry voice.

She noticed the way he addressed her and thought it was rather an impertinence on his part. Then she remembered that if he called

Nanette by her name without a prefix, it was obvious that he would do the same to her, although she had not expected it.

They drove along in silence. Then, because she could not bear the suspense, Prunella said in a very different voice from the one she had used before:

"It may be . . . wrong of me . . . to ask you . . . but . . . I have to know . . . have you . . . sold the Van Dykes . . . and if so . . . how many?"

Once again the Earl turned to look at her, and because she was embarrassed she would not meet his eyes, but stared ahead at the faded cushions in the carriage.

"I am not going to answer that question," he said after a perceptible pause. "I shall leave you guessing, or perhaps we might discuss it tomorrow night when you dine with me."

"I cannot think why you should be so mysterious about it," Prunella said crossly.

She had the feeling that he was teasing her, and she told herself that the sale of the Van Dykes was not something that should be treated lightly or as a joke.

"There are other things I want to talk to you about," the Earl said, "but perhaps the most important is what you intend to do about yourself now that you are free of the responsibility of Winslow Hall. And of course, what you intend to do about Nanette. She will moulder away at the Manor without any amusement or local entertainments except that, I am told, you occasionally have the riotous gaiety of tea at the Vicarage."

"Who has been talking to you? Who has been telling you these things?" Prunella asked sharply.

The Earl made a gesture with his hands.

"The world and his wife, or rather everybody I have talked to since I came home."

"Then I wish you would mind your own business!" Prunella ejaculated. "What Nanette and I do is not your affair, My Lord, and we are perfectly happy."

"Then you must be a fat cow, chewing the cud, and I do not need to be told that that is untrue, while what you are saying is!"

He saw Prunella purse her lips together, and he smiled as he continued:

"I am quite sure that Nanette will find Little Stodbury a very poor substitute for London, and if you are content as you say, then it is certainly time you were shaken out of your dream-world, which has nothing to offer except perhaps a soporific against suicide!"

"You are certainly very eloquent on the subject, My Lord," Prunella said scathingly.

"As for it not being my business, you have already asked for my help," the Earl continued. "I am quite certain that my nephew, whatever he is like, would seem to Nanette like all the heroes of mythology and the Prince Charming of every fairy-tale, after a few lonely weeks in the gloom of the Manor."

"I will not have you talking like this about my

home!" Prunella objected.

"What I am saying is the truth and you know it! What you and I have to decide, Prunella, is how we can bring life and laughter into the lives of two forlorn maidens."

"I should think Your Lordship had plenty to occupy you at the moment without troubling yourself about us," Prunella answered. "You will soon forget Little Stodbury when you return to London."

"Who said I was going to London?"

"I cannot believe that, after the way you have described my home, you will find yours any more enlivening."

"On the contrary, I find the Hall absorbing," the Earl said. "But then, as you have discovered for yourself, there is a great deal to do both in the house and on the Estate."

By this time they were passing through the village and the Manor was not far ahead.

"Are you going to help me, as you suggested before," the Earl asked, "or fight me?"

"The place is yours."

"I am getting rather tired of being continually engaged in a pitched battle."

Prunella turned to look at him in surprise.

"A pitched battle?" she questioned.

"I am not so obtuse as not to be aware that you dislike and despise me," he said. "You are merely waiting for me to commit some unforgivable sin so that you can vent your righteous wrath upon me."

"That is not true!" Prunella exclaimed. "And talking in that exaggerated manner does not help our relationship."

"So we have one! That really does surprise me!" the Earl remarked.

She felt as if they were duelling and she had given him an opening which he had not failed to take.

"I think, My Lord," she said, "that you are making far more out of this than is necessary. I want to help you to do what is right as regards the people on your Estate, and I want you to help me be rid of your nephew Pascoe. Surely we can do these two things together without fighting?"

"What you mean is being permanently at each other's throats," the Earl said, "and that, my prudish little Prunella, is something you have been doing ever since I returned."

She would have spoken, but he held up his hand to interrupt her.

"All right, what I did when you were too young to know what I was doing has shocked you, and I think, if you are honest, you will admit that you have added my sins to your mother's, which I consider extremely unfair."

As he spoke Prunella had bent her head, and he went on in a very much quieter and more gentle tone:

"Suppose for the moment, Prunella, we bury the hatchet? I need your help and I will try to help you. That is, at least, a basis for a relationship that need not be so acrimonious as it has been up to this moment. Do you agree?"

He held out his hand as he spoke, and almost despite herself and because she could not find words in which to answer him, Prunella put hers in it.

She had taken off her gloves when she was talking to Nanny, and, because she had been so agitated by the Earl's visit and by his request to drive home with her, she had not replaced them.

Now as his fingers closed over hers, she felt the hard strength of them and it gave her a very strange feeling.

She could not explain it except that she supposed she had never been touched in such an intimate way by a man before, and it was different from what she had expected.

"I am . . . sorry if I . . . have been . . . disagreeable, My Lord."

As the words came from her lips she thought that she sounded like Nanette, and she was sure that if she looked up at the Earl she would see him smiling, thinking he had won a small victory.

Instead he said very quietly:

"If you are sorry, then I too am sorry that I am not what you expected."

Just then they turned in at the drive to the Manor.

As they did so, the Earl raised Prunella's hand to his lips and kissed it.

Chapter Four

Driving beside Nanette towards the Hall, Prunella had an unaccountable feeling in her breast which she could not explain.

She supposed it was because she felt embarrassed at seeing the Earl after their conversation of yesterday, but she was aware that it was also due to her appearance.

Although she had protested violently, Nanette had insisted on her trying on a number of her gowns to see which was the most becoming.

"I will not go anywhere dressed in white like a débutante!" Prunella had said firmly. "I am nearly twenty-two, and, as you pointed out when you were angry with me, I am well on the way to being an old maid."

"I only said that because you upset me," Nanette answered. "You may be older in years, Prunella, but sometimes I feel that you are younger than I. But then I went away to School, and I have also been to London."

Prunella thought that was very near the truth.

Nanette sometimes talked in a worldly-wise, sophisticated manner which left her gasping.

Then she would remember humbly how little she knew of the world outside Little Stodbury.

Nanette's new gowns were lovely, elegant, and had cost what seemed to Prunella to be an astronomical amount of money.

"I thought you would be shocked at my extravagance," she said, "but Godmama said firmly that first appearances are very important and she would not take me anywhere until I was dressed in a way she considered suitable for an heiress."

"I think that is rather an unladylike way of talking," Prunella said. "Mama always said that ladies and gentlemen never spoke of money."

Nanette laughed scornfully.

"If that was true they certainly did not live in Little Stodbury!"

She smiled before she went on:

"You know as well as I do, Prunella, that ever since I have been home, conversation has been everlastingly about the lack of money at the Hall! While in London, although they talk of it in low voices, people are continually telling each other what somebody else is worth."

"I prefer to think about people's characters," Prunella said airily.

Nanette gave a little cry and clapped her hands.

"That is exactly what I have been asking you to do where Pascoe is concerned. He has an adorable character — kind, gentle, considerate, and you forget all that simply because he has not a lot of guineas to jingle in his pocket."

Prunella thought a little ruefully that she had certainly fallen into that trap! It was almost as if she were duelling with the Earl in words rather than with her own sister.

She had the feeling that the authority which she had always had over Nanette was slipping away, and it made her more determined than ever that she would not wear white, because she did not wish to appear the same age as her sister.

"Would you consider white and silver?" Nanette asked, looking into a wardrobe that was packed with gowns, each of which was prettier than the last.

Prunella shook her head.

"I will wear my black gown, and as a concession to the occasion I will wear Mama's diamond necklace."

"You will look like a crow!" Nanette said rudely.

Then she gave an exclamation.

"I have it! I have exactly the right gown for you!"

She opened another cupboard where Charity had put the gowns that could not be squeezed into her big wardrobe.

Prunella waited, but very expectantly.

Being a woman, she naturally longed to have lovely clothes to wear as Nanette did, but the truth was that she had spent more than she could afford on restoring the Salon at the Hall.

'I suppose I could always draw on my capital,' she had thought, and could not help knowing how horrified her father would have been at the idea.

Nanette came back from the cupboard with a

gown that was even more elaborate than the ones at which they had been looking, but instead of being white it was a pale, misty blue.

"Godmama and I chose this in an artificial light," she said, "and when I put it on it did not suit me, so I have never worn it."

Prunella knew, however, that it was exactly what she wanted! The blue was very soft and at night it deepened a little so that it looked like the sky on a misty day.

When she put it on it fitted her almost exactly, and made her look not only different from what she had ever looked before but very much lovelier.

While Nanette had golden hair that was the colour of ripening corn, Prunella's was fair but with a touch of brown in it, and her eyes instead of being blue were cloudy grey.

Yet her skin, like Nanette's, was dazzlingly white and had a translucence which, although she was unaware of it, made it glow almost like a pearl.

The blacks and greys she had worn for over a year had seemed to take the sparkle from her eyes, and the way her gowns were made had prevented anyone from being aware of the grace of her figure.

Now the close-fitting bodice, the sweeping line from the high breast to the hem, gave her an elegance and at the same time something classical which was almost Grecian.

"You look lovely!" Nanette exclaimed when

Prunella went into her room to see if she was ready.

She looked her sister up and down, then added:

"Do you know, Prunella, if the London dress-makers saw you, they would say you 'paid with dressing,' and that is the truth."

"I think you are speaking metaphorically," Prunella replied, "but what I am wondering is how much it would cost in hard cash."

Nanette laughed.

"Whatever it costs, I am going to see that in the future you are properly gowned, and you know, dearest, that I will pay for anything you cannot afford, considering you gave me all the money Mama left you."

Prunella stiffened and did not reply.

Nanette looked at her. Then she said:

"People in London talk about Mama without looking shocked. All the old Dowagers told me how beautiful she was, and although I think it is unlikely if she were alive that they would invite her to their parties, they never said anything un-pleasant in my hearing."

Prunella was determined not to discuss her mother, so she said quickly:

"We must hurry and finish dressing or we will be late. And you know as well as I do that Mrs. Carter is not a very good cook, and if she gets agitated the dinner will be inedible."

"I am ready," Nanette said. "Do you think I look nice?"

"Nice" was not the word to describe her.

In her white gown trimmed round the shoulders and hem with shadow lace, she looked like a Princess in a fairy-story. To add to the illusion, she wore a little wreath of blue forget-me-nots in her hair and a necklace of small turquoises to match.

Prunella was certain that the forget-me-nots had a special meaning but she did not comment on them, and she told her sister the truth, that she did indeed look lovely.

As she turned away, Nanette enquired:

"What are you going to wear over your gown to drive to the Hall?"

"I have my velvet cloak downstairs."

"That old thing!" Nanette exclaimed scornfully. "You must have one of my scarves. There is a very pretty one here trimmed with maribou which will keep you warm."

She wrapped it round Prunella's shoulders as she spoke, when she gave a little sigh.

"I wish we were going to dine with the Earl in London, then on to a Ball where I could dance with Pascoe."

Prunella thought it was a mistake to answer this and she moved towards the stairs. Because her gown was so elegant and made of such expensive material she felt as if she were floating rather than walking.

Dawson was waiting for them outside with the closed carriage and they drove away. The sun was sinking, the shadows had grown longer and darker on the lawn, and the rooks were going to roost in the oak trees in the Park.

"Are you excited, Prunella?" Nanette asked. "After all, although you disapprove of the Earl, he is a man, and surely it must be thrilling for you to talk to him rather than to the Vicar, who is the only man we ever see in Little Stodbury."

As it happened, Prunella was thinking very much the same thing, and when they arrived at the Hall she thought that for Nanette's sake she would try to be more pleasant to the Earl than she had been on previous occasions when they met.

They alighted, then as Prunella walked up the old stone steps that she had climbed for so many years of her life, she looked with astonishment at the figure standing at the top of them.

She had expected to see Carter, who was very old and rheumaticky and, because his feet hurt him, always shuffled about in bedroom slippers.

But the servant waiting for them at the open door was extremely impressive-looking. He was bearded and wore a turban on his head.

Prunella recognised him as a Sikh. As he salaamed to them politely, Nanette stared at him in astonishment and whispered:

"The Earl must have brought him back from India."

"Yes, of course," Prunella replied. "But he looks very strange at the Hall."

The Indian servant walked ahead and to Prunella's surprise opened the door of the Salon.

She had expected that, as the Earl was alone, he would be using the Library, where they had talked the first day that she had come to the Hall to find him.

Now as she walked into what had always been known as the Gold Salon she saw that the Holland covers had gone, the curtains were drawn, the chandeliers were lit, and the walls, which she had restored, were revealed in all their glory.

This was the most important room in the whole house and had been designed by Inigo Jones with the help of his pupil John Webb, and it was in Prunella's mind the most beautiful room she had ever imagined.

After a burst water-pipe from the floor above had damaged it, she had searched through all the old designs and found the actual sketches which Inigo Jones had made for the room.

Following them, she had had the walls painted white and had regilded the huge swags of fruit, flowers, and foliage in different shades of gold.

Fortunately, the paintings had not been damaged, nor the console tables with porphyry tops designed by William Kent. The curtains of crimson velvet matched the furniture and it now looked exactly, Prunella thought, as it had when it had first been completed.

She was so intent on looking at the room itself, and glancing up at the painted ceiling with its gods and goddesses depicted against a blue sky, that it was difficult for a moment to focus her eyes on the Earl.

Then as she saw him moving across the room to greet them she was aware that behind him there was another man and with a start she recognised Pascoe Lowes.

Even if she had not done so, she would have been made aware that he was there by the sudden exclamation of sheer delight which came from Nanette's lips.

"Pascoe!" she murmured rapturously.

Then Prunella heard the Earl saying:

"Let me welcome you, Prunella, and tell you what a pleasure it is that you and Nanette, together with my nephew Pascoe, should be my first guests on my return home."

With an effort Prunella remembered to curtsey.

Then before she could speak she heard Nanette say to the Earl:

"Thank you, thank you! I knew this would be an exciting evening!"

She was looking at him as if he had given her a present of inestimable worth.

Then, as if she could not wait, she ran from his side towards Pascoe and her hands were in his.

The Earl's eyes were on Prunella's face and he said in a low voice that only she could hear:

"Before you start finding fault, let me say quickly that I have a reason for including my nephew in this particular party."

"I hope it is a good one!" Prunella said repressively.

"It is," the Earl replied, "but first may I tell

you how attractive you look? It is the first time I have seen you fashionably gowned, and as we are always so frank with each other, let me add that it is a very great improvement!"

Prunella looked at him angrily, thinking that what he was saying was an impertinence.

Then as she saw the twinkle in his eyes and knew that he was teasing her, she thought that if she allowed herself to be provoked by what he was saying, it would seem childish.

"Nanette has already made me humbly conscious that I am a country mouse, My Lord."

"If that is true, it is a mouse with very extravagant taste," the Earl said.

Prunella looked at him in surprise, thinking that he was referring to her gown, but he added quietly:

"I thought it appropriate that we should be in this room tonight, considering how much it owes to you."

Because it was something she had not expected him to say, she merely looked round, wondering if he was rebuking her for spending so much on just one room when it was unlikely that he would ever be able to repay her.

Then, struggling to find the right words, she answered:

"I think this room . . . is one of the finest Inigo Jones ever designed . . . it belongs . . . not only to the Hall . . . My Lord, but to posterity."

"I am sure you are right, Prunella, but at the moment I am very grateful that it belongs to me."

There was an undoubted note of sincerity in the Earl's voice, to which Prunella was unable to reply, for at that moment Pascoe had detached himself from Nanette who had been talking to him eagerly, to say:

"Forgive me, Miss Broughton. It is a very great pleasure to see you again."

"Thank you," Prunella answered, but she had stiffened at his approach and her tone was cold.

"Because this is a house-warming," the Earl said, "I insist that we celebrate with champagne and that you drink my health."

As he spoke, the Indian servant came into the room with a silver tray on which reposed a bottle of champagne in a silver wine-cooler.

He set it down on the table and when they each had a glass in their hands the Earl raised his.

"To Winslow Hall!" he said. "And to its Guardian Angel, who has preserved it for my home-coming and to whom I am overwhelmingly grateful."

His toast took Prunella by surprise and she felt the colour flooding into her face as they drank to her.

Then Nanette said:

"You see, Prunella, all the time and effort you put into the Hall is really appreciated! Is that not so, My Lord?"

"I am indeed very grateful," the Earl replied, "and every day I find new instances of your sister's generosity."

105

Because she was afraid he was resenting that she had done so much, Prunella blushed again, and to change the subject she said to Pascoe in a more pleasant way than she would have done otherwise:

"Did you remember your uncle after not seeing him for so many years?"

"Of course I remembered him!" Pascoe replied. "How could I forget anyone who always seemed to me to be a dashing hero and was made all the more so as everybody spoke of him with bated breath?"

"On the contrary, Prunella will tell you that I was talked about with horror!" the Earl remarked.

"Only because they had nothing else to talk about!" Nanette said quickly. "And now you are home it will be quite easy for you to earn yourself a halo, and then the past will be forgotten."

The Earl laughed.

"You are very encouraging, Nanette, and I shall look to you to help me on the upward path which I have a feeling is going to be a somewhat wearisome climb from the Prodigal Son."

"We will help you," Nanette said with a smile, "will we not, Pascoe?"

She held out her hand as she spoke and he took it in both of his.

Prunella turned away with a little flounce of her skirt. She walked to the table that stood between two of the windows and looked down at its contents.

It contained a collection of snuff-boxes which had belonged to the Earl's father and grandfather. She had arranged them against a background of new blue velvet which replaced one which had become faded and dusty.

The Earl went to her side to ask:

"Are you counting to see if I have already disposed of my most valuable possessions?"

Prunella started as she remembered that they were on her list of things which she had thought were the most saleable.

She knew it would be a great pity to part with them. At the same time, they were not so old or so unique as many of the other treasures in the house.

"Actually I was thinking how attractive they look," she replied.

"At the same time, you were ready to let them go," he said, almost as if he wanted to force her into an admission.

"Everything is precious when it means something personal," she answered, "and therefore I know how difficult it must be for you to make a choice."

"Are you really considering my feelings in the matter?"

"Of course I am!" Prunella replied. "These are your possessions and you have known them all your life. Naturally it will be hard for you to part with even one of them."

"I am glad that you think of me like that," the Earl said. "I had the feeling that you thought I

107

was ready to sell anything and everything to raise enough money to provide me with the amusements that I must obviously crave after being in exile for so many years."

Because this was so near the truth as to be uncomfortable, Prunella walked to the window.

"I see you have started work on the garden," she said. "Have you been able to find somebody to help old Ives?"

"Ives tells me he wishes to retire," the Earl replied, "and I do not think he is capable of working more than an hour or so a day."

"That is true," Prunella agreed, "but he has done his best."

"I appreciate that," the Earl said, "and I have found a cottage for him."

"Found a cottage?" Prunella questioned. "What is wrong with the house in which he is now living? He has been there for twenty years, since he became Head Gardener, and he would not wish to leave."

"I have spoken to Ives," the Earl answered, "and he quite understands that I should require his house for the man who is to replace him. I am sure Ives will be quite comfortable as soon as I have done up the cottage I have chosen for him."

With great difficulty Prunella prevented herself from asking which one.

She had an uneasy feeling that the Earl was deliberately tantalising her by telling her of the innovations he was making without being exactly explicit.

'He wants to make me curious,' she thought. 'He wants me to appear to interfere so that he can tell me he intends to do what he wants without my assistance.'

She turned round from the window to look to where Nanette was talking intimately with Pascoe.

They were close to each other, and any on-looker would have realised as they looked at each other that they were in love.

"My nephew arrived today," the Earl said quietly at Prunella's side. "As you told me to expect, he is a handsome and attractive young man."

"Superficially," Prunella replied.

"He has told me quite frankly of his circumstances," the Earl said, "and I find it difficult to understand how my brother-in-law could have made such a mess of his affairs. I always believed him to be a rich man."

"Your father believed the same thing."

"Which is unfortunate for me, as it is for my nephew."

"I asked your help," Prunella said in a low voice.

"Which I am prepared to give you," the Earl answered, "if you can prove to me that it is for your sister's happiness that they should be parted, and of course for my nephew's."

Prunella looked at him indignantly.

"Are you suggesting for one moment," she asked, "that you will encourage that dressed-up Dandy to marry my sister for her money?"

"Certainly not, if that is what he is doing," the Earl replied firmly.

"Then tell him he is to leave her alone."

"Is there any other man in her life?"

"No, not at the moment. But if your nephew is not there, I will make sure that she finds one."

"How can you do that?"

"By letting her go back to London, and even taking her there if necessary."

The Earl smiled.

"I have a feeling that is an original idea where you are concerned, and why not? It would do you good to go to London, and I think it might widen your horizons quite considerably."

"I am not concerned with myself, My Lord," Prunella snapped. "I am thinking of Nanette."

"While I," the Earl replied, "although you may not believe me, am thinking of you as well as of Nanette and Pascoe."

The dinner was a more enjoyable meal than Prunella had expected, and certainly it was a surprising one.

To begin with, there were two Indian servants to wait on them, and as soon as the food was brought to the table she knew that it had not been cooked by Mrs. Carter.

Not only was it delicious, but the wines that accompanied it were superb, some of which Prunella had never tasted before.

The Earl set out to make the dinner stimulating mentally as well as physically.

Prunella had already realised that he was cleverer and more intelligent than she had expected him to be, and now he made them laugh with his stories of India and of the long, rather dismal voyage home.

Because he was talking animatedly, Pascoe forgot to drawl in what was the fashionable manner amongst the Bucks of St. James's Street, and tried to cap his uncle's stories in a way which entranced Nanette and even made Prunella laugh despite herself.

Time seemed to speed past, and when Prunella rose to leave the gentlemen to their port, Nanette, as soon as they were outside the Dining-Room, slipped her hand into hers.

"Oh, Prunella, what fun it is, and I have never known Pascoe to be so amusing. Even you had to laugh at his jokes."

They reached the Hall, and when Nanette would have gone towards the Salon, Prunella said:

"I want to go upstairs. You need not come with me if you do not want to."

"Of course I will come with you," Nanette replied.

They walked up the staircase, but when Nanette expected her sister to move towards one of the State Bedrooms she went in the opposite direction and a moment or two later they entered the Picture-Gallery.

Prunella stood still in the doorway.

Then as she looked down the length of the Gallery she felt a constriction in her heart, as if somebody had stabbed her.

Mrs. Goodwin had been right!

The paintings had been taken down from the walls and she could see some of them, she could not count how many, stacked on the floor, and there was not one Van Dyke hanging in its place.

She did not say anything, she only turned and walked back down the stairs and into the Salon, feeling as if the house itself had fallen down and was lying in ruins at her feet.

"I know you are upset!" Nanette cried. "But you know as well as I do, Prunella, he had to sell something to pay for his horses, those funny-looking servants, and the repairs he is doing to the cottages."

She paused before she added:

"You should be pleased about that, at any rate. You have always worried yourself silly about the old people and you have spent all your own money on them."

Prunella found it impossible to answer.

She was only feeling that in some way the Earl had deceived her by being so pleasant in asking for her advice and promising to help her about Pascoe.

She had thought, perhaps foolishly, that he intended to do what she wished and sell some of the treasures but not the Van Dykes.

"They are his paintings," she tried to tell herself, "and it is for him to make the decision . . . not me."

But somehow she still felt betrayed and cheated, and once again she was hating him.

"Oh, Prunella, do stop looking so upset," Nanette pleaded. "You will spoil the whole evening. I am enjoying myself, and it is so wonderful to have Pascoe here. I have been thinking about him all day and how miserable I am without him."

"I will tell you what we will do," Prunella said.

She had found her voice at last and it seemed somehow unlike her own.

"What is that?" Nanette asked.

"We will go to London! There is not much of the Season left. In fact, most people are leaving. But you want to buy me new clothes, you want to see your friends, and I am sure some of them will still be there! At least we can get away from here."

Nanette looked at her in astonishment.

Prunella knew she was running away from something which hurt her unbearably, but she could not stand by and see it happening without protesting!

And that she had no right to do.

When they left for London the next morning Nanette was complaining volubly.

"I cannot understand why you are in such a hurry, Prunella," she had said. "Pascoe is staying with his uncle until tomorrow, and I wanted to see him."

"We are leaving!" Prunella said firmly. "And because I cannot leave you alone in the house, you will have to come with me."

"Of course I am prepared to come with you, and I want to go to London," Nanette replied, "but not in such a hurry!"

Charity said the same thing.

"Good gracious me, Miss Prunella, you've sat here year after year without a word passing your lips, and now you're leaving before I've even got me breath!"

Prunella was adamant, and because she had so little packing to do it was easy for everybody in the house to push Nanette's gowns into several trunks, and they were on their way before noon.

When they had reached home the night before, Prunella had been unable to sleep.

All she could think of was the long Gallery with its bare walls, the shadows in the corners seeming as dark and dismal as the misery within her heart.

The loss of the paintings made her feel again, and even more strongly, that the Earl had deceived her in being so pleasant, thanking her for what she had done for the Hall, when all the time he was doing the one thing that she had begged him not to do.

She felt as if the portraits of his ancestors had called out to her to save them, and she had failed, while treasures which were far less important were still in their places.

'I expect they too will soon go,' she thought bitterly. 'They will be sold to pay for servants, to buy horses, and doubtless for the repairs to the peach- and grape-houses.'

"How can he be so stupid," she raged in the darkness of the night, "not to know what is part of history and what are unessential luxuries?"

When the Earl and Pascoe had joined them in the Salon she had felt an irresistible impulse to rage at him; to tell him in front of the two young people how his successors in the future would look back and curse him for despoiling what should have become theirs.

Then she told herself that that would only be to behave just as his father had behaved, which had driven "Master Gerald" away in the first place.

She knew that neither Nanette nor Pascoe would understand how much she minded, and they would be shocked if she behaved in an un-controlled manner or in any way unlike her usual self.

She therefore sat stiff and unsmiling while the others laughed and talked, and long before Nanette was ready to leave, she rose to say they should go home.

"Oh, not yet, Prunella! What is the hurry?"

"Old Dawson is not used to being kept out late," Prunella replied with the first excuse that came to her mind.

"I thought of that," the Earl said. "Actually I told him to go home before dinner and I have arranged to send you back in my carriage."

"In your carriage?" Prunella echoed.

"I was surprised to find that my father had anything so comfortable," the Earl answered, "but of course later I must buy a Cabriolet, which is more up-to-date and better sprung. To-night Jim will drive you home and I promise he will get you there safely."

"How wonderful of you to think of it!" Nanette cried. "I promised I would show Pascoe the Library. We will not be long."

They disappeared together before Prunella could expostulate, and as soon as they had gone the Earl said:

"What has upset you?"

"Nothing," she answered untruthfully. "I am just anxious, as you well know, that Nanette should not become more involved and enamoured of your nephew than she is already."

"She is a very lovely girl," the Earl said reflectively.

"In which case you will realise that I do not wish her to throw herself away on a man who is not worthy of her."

The Earl's lips twisted in a rather cynical smile.

"If marriage was always based on worthiness, there would be very few weddings."

"That may be your idea," Prunella said scathingly, "but you must understand that as Nanette has no parents I am her Guardian."

"You have a propensity for taking on other people's burdens," the Earl said, but he did not make it sound a virtue, and Prunella replied:

"I have to do what I believe to be my duty."

The Earl laughed.

"Duty! How I loathe that word! It was drummed into me when I was a child that it was my 'duty' to do this and my 'duty' to do that. It was a word my father was very fond of, and so, I am certain, was yours."

"A lot of people, My Lord, are very conscious of their responsibilities in life."

"And some are not," the Earl replied. "Oh, well, happiness is where you find it. I may be wrong, but I have a feeling that is something you have not yet discovered."

Prunella looked at him in a startled fashion.

"Why should you think I am unhappy?"

"Are you?"

"That is not a question I want to answer."

"I should like you to answer it — not to me, but to yourself — because real happiness, Prunella, and remember this, is enjoying life to the full, and that is something that I have a feeling you have not begun to do and have no idea how to start."

Prunella lifted her chin a little higher.

"I think, My Lord, you are trying to make me dissatisfied with my life as it is," she said, "and I cannot quite understand your motives for doing so."

"Perhaps I am merely opening the door to new interests, new adventures," the Earl said. "I would like, Prunella, to show you a very different world from the one in which you have incarcerated yourself like a small snail carrying its house upon its back."

"I cannot imagine what you are trying to say," Prunella said crushingly, "and now, My Lord, I think it is definitely time for Nanette and me to go home."

She rose to her feet as she spoke, and as she did so Nanette and Pascoe came back into the room.

There was a rapt look on their faces which aroused in Prunella an uneasy suspicion that Nanette had been kissed.

She could hardly believe that her sister would behave in such a reprehensible fashion, yet the suspicion persisted all the way home.

Nanette sat very quietly in the corner of the carriage, not talking, as she usually did, her eyes shining, a smile on her lips, and her hands clasped together as if in a kind of ecstasy.

Only when Prunella told her that they were leaving for London the next morning did she rouse herself to protest and argue, but it was to no avail.

When they reached London, Prunella drove to a quiet, old-fashioned Hotel where their father had occasionally stayed when obliged to visit London for a Regimental dinner or some reason connected with his official duties in the County.

When Prunella explained who they were, the Manager greeted them effusively and offered his deepest condolences on Sir Roderick's death.

They had been shown into a large, gloomy Suite furnished with heavy mahogany and with two impersonal, rather cheerless bedrooms opening out of it.

Nanette threw herself down in a chair to say:

"Well, we have come to London when I never expected it. At the same time, I cannot think what you are up to, Prunella."

"Why should I be 'up to' anything?" Prunella enquired. "It is an expression I do not care for."

"Because I know you so well," Nanette replied. "You hate London and like being at the Manor, bossing everybody about . . ."

She stopped suddenly.

"Now I know why you have come away!" she exclaimed. "It is because you are piqued with the Earl for taking over your position as 'Lady Bountiful'!"

"That is not true," Prunella objected.

"But of course it is!" Nanette replied. "You have had everything your own way for so long, running the Hall as well as the Manor, having everybody on the Estate saying you were an 'Angel of Mercy.' Now they are all fawning on the Earl. Oh, poor Prunella, of course you mind!"

"I do not! I do not mind in the slightest! And what you are saying is quite untrue!"

Then as Prunella spoke she knew that her protest was half-hearted and that Nanette had unerringly put her finger on the real reason for their departure.

Chapter Five

Pascoe walked into the Breakfast-Room and as the Earl looked up from the table he knew something was wrong.

"What has happened?" he enquired.

"They are leaving for London this morning!"

"How do you know?"

"I have just had a note which Nanette sent me by a groom. She says her sister is determined to go to London, and of course it is to be rid of me."

The Earl smiled.

"I think I must also take some of the blame."

"You?" his nephew enquired.

"I told Prunella last night that it would be good for her to widen her horizons."

"I am not concerned with what Miss Prunella does, but with her sister."

"That is obvious."

Pascoe walked to the sideboard where a whole array of silver dishes were waiting for him to make a choice of what he would eat.

He took the heavy crested lids off them, one after another, then in a petulant manner helped himself to a slice of cold ham and sat down at the table.

He looked at his uncle and asked:

"What is to stop us from going to London too?"

"Nothing, as far as I am concerned," the Earl replied.

Pascoe's expression lightened.

"Then we will leave immediately," he said, "and the first thing we will do is to buy you some new clothes."

The Earl laughed.

"I am well aware that I need them."

"You most certainly do! If you are playing the part of the Prodigal Son, you are not eating husks — you are wearing them!"

The Earl laughed again.

"What I have is the best that Calcutta could provide."

"Then I am sorry for those who have to live in India," his nephew retorted.

"I am not as clothes-conscious as you, my dear boy, but I agree with you that I need a new wardrobe, and I do not wish my old friends to be ashamed of me."

Pascoe glanced at him slyly.

"If you are speaking of your erstwhile ladyfriends, they will be a bit long in the tooth by this time."

"I can always look at their daughters," the Earl replied.

There was silence as Pascoe ate a few mouthfuls of the ham, then pushed aside his plate.

"I have not had a chance to talk to you, Uncle

Gerald, but you know that I wish to marry Nanette?"

"I certainly had that impression," the Earl remarked drily.

"The difficulty is that her sister, who I gather is in the position of being her Guardian, is violently opposed to me. I have done my best, but I doubt if I made the slightest impression on her conviction that I am a fortune-hunter."

The Earl sat back in his chair.

"Is that what you are?"

"Of course I am — or I was," Pascoe replied frankly. "It has been drummed into me by father and mother ever since I left Eton that if I am to keep the Estate going and live in a Castle, I have to marry money."

"And that is what you wish to do now?"

"I want to marry Nanette, which is a very different thing," Pascoe answered. "No-one will believe me, least of all her sister, but I would still want to marry her if she had not a penny. I love her! She is the most adorable person I have ever met in my whole life."

The Earl thought for a moment. Then he said:

"If it is true, then it looks as if you will have to wait until she is twenty-one."

"I am prepared to do that, even though it will be hell for both of us," Pascoe answered, "and especially for me, knowing that her mind is being poisoned against me by her sister, and doubtless also by you."

"I have not condemned you," the Earl replied

mildly. "After all, why should I? You are very much like what I was at your age."

"Am I really?" Pascoe asked eagerly. "You certainly had a reputation for being very wild and doing outrageous things, but I never heard you referred to as a 'fortune-hunter.' "

"I suppose I always considered my father rich enough for me to avoid that stigma," the Earl said, "but I certainly sowed my wild oats and enjoyed doing so."

"Which resulted in your being more or less exiled for fourteen years," Pascoe said. "That is something I do not wish to happen to me."

"You might enjoy India."

"No! I wish to live in England, in London part of the time, and in the country if I can afford horses to hunt and to race, and to entertain."

Pascoe gave an exasperated exclamation as he added:

"But what is the use? I am in debt and I have nothing to offer Nanette except my heart, which will certainly not fetch much on the open market."

"I should have thought that its value was what she put on it," the Earl said quietly.

Pascoe rose from the table and walked across the room.

"If I could persuade that damned sister of hers to give me a chance, we could be married by Christmas, and I swear to you I would make her a very good husband."

The Earl was watching his nephew and

thinking that he could understand any young woman of Nanette's age being fascinated by him.

He was undoubtedly very handsome, but, what was more important, his expression was open and frank and when he smiled it reached his eyes.

The Earl was a good judge of men and he thought to himself that his nephew, while undoubtedly spoilt by too much adulation from the fair sex, had certain qualities that were important in a man.

"I suppose what I should say to you," he said aloud, "is that if you really care for Nanette you should be prepared to fight for her. If not, drop her, and look elsewhere."

"I have no wish to do that."

"Then as I say — you must fight!"

"But how? How can I manage to marry her when that dragon stands between us?"

He sat down again at the table and leant towards his uncle.

"Help me, Uncle Gerald. Heaven knows you have had enough experience with women! Convince Miss Prunella that I am not as black as I am painted. Surely that is not too much to ask you?"

"I thought when you arrived here," the Earl answered, "that you intended to ask me for a loan."

Pascoe gave him a somewhat rueful smile.

"I thought of it when I heard you had returned

124

from India," he said. "But when I saw you wearing those rusty old clothes and heard of the condition of the Winslow Estate, I knew there was no hope of any financial assistance."

He bent forward again.

"But you can help me in a very different and much more fundamental way. Will you try?"

"I must point out to you that the lady in question has an aversion to me which is deep-rooted," the Earl replied. "All her life she has been shocked by knowing that when I left this country I did not travel alone. She also berates me for allowing the Estate to fall into disrepair, and now for selling the Van Dykes."

"Have you sold them?" Pascoe asked. "Well, I do not blame you. Those old jossers on the walls had their good time when they were alive, and there is no reason why they should not contribute to your enjoyment now that they are dead!"

The Earl laughed.

"I think if you said that to Prunella she would have a stroke!"

"Let her!" Pascoe said. "I only wish I had a few Van Dykes of my own, but doubtless you remember that the paintings at the Castle were a pretty mouldy lot."

"Thinking of your father's Estate," the Earl said, "I cannot help feeling that if it was properly managed it might do well. After all, the soil in Huntingdonshire is good."

"I know nothing about it."

"Then why not learn?"

His nephew looked at the Earl in astonishment.

"Are you suggesting that I should manage the Estate myself?"

"Why not? Your father, as you told me yesterday, is now incapable of exercising any control over it, and I am quite certain that your mother would welcome any interest you showed in what after all is your inheritance."

Pascoe digested this with a frown between his eyes.

"Now that I think of it," he said, "I have often thought that everything was done in a very old-fashioned way, and there was no possibility of introducing new ideas, which of course my father would never consider."

"When he dies, the responsibility will be yours," the Earl said. "Think it over, Pascoe. I cannot help feeling that there are things which you and I have not yet discovered about the countryside, and which should receive our attention."

"I will tell you what I have discovered," Pascoe replied grimly, "and that is crumbling farms, broken-down cottages, pensioners too old to work, and of course no money to take on extra labourers."

"All in all, a depressingly dismal picture," the Earl remarked.

"I would not know where to begin, unless I had the money to put things right," Pascoe said.

"Which brings us back to Nanette."

"Dammit all, I will marry her, however her sister tries to stop me!" Pascoe exclaimed. "And what is more, if she does marry me, we will make a go of the old place together. It has always meant something to me, I suppose, because it is my home."

"I wish you luck."

"And you will help me with Miss Prunella?"

"I will think about it," the Earl answered. "In the meantime, if we are going to London I had best order my Phaeton. I presume you would wish to drive there as swiftly as my new team will carry us?"

"But of course," Pascoe agreed, his eyes lighting up.

Prunella was sitting in the dark and rather dreary Sitting-Room of their Hotel Suite when Nanette came into it from her bedroom.

"I feel so mean, dearest Prunella," she said, "leaving you alone, but I did not like to ask Godmama to invite you a second time. You know how she dislikes too many unattached women."

"Of course I understand," Prunella replied, "and your friends have been very kind to me. I had a delightful luncheon yesterday with that nice Lady Dobson, and I enjoyed the other evening with our cousins."

"That is more than I did," Nanette replied. "I thought they were a stuffy lot, and all they wanted to talk about, if you had let them, was Mama."

"I realised that," Prunella said, "and I thought

it was very tactless of Cousin Cecilia to keep referring to her."

"I think she is too old to know any better," Nanette said. "But it was certainly an evening we need not repeat."

Prunella gave a little sigh.

Ever since they had come to London she had been scouring her memory to recall not only their relations but friends of their father's with whom he had kept in touch.

Fortunately Nanette had found quite a number of the acquaintances she had made in the Season who had still not left for the country. They had welcomed her effusively and invited her to dinner and to parties.

The only difficulty was that they did not want two unattached girls, and Prunella was very anxious not to make Nanette feel that she was an encumbrance.

The first thing they had done immediately on arrival was to search Bond Street for new gowns. Nanette was determined that her sister should be as well dressed as she was herself, and she swept aside all Prunella's protests and chose so many different garments for her that she lost count.

"I am not going to be ashamed of you," Nanette said fiercely, "and that means it is going to cost money! It does not matter who pays; whether it is you or I, you still have to look right, and that is all that matters."

Prunella certainly looked right at the moment,

wearing an evening-gown of pale green which seemed somehow to be reflected in her eyes.

It made her skin look even more dazzlingly white than usual, and Nanette said penitently:

"I ought not to leave you behind, but, dearest, what can I do?"

"I shall be all right," Prunella said. "I only put on this gown because Charity wanted to be sure it fitted me in case I wanted to wear it on a more important occasion."

"You look far too lovely to dine alone," Nanette said, "but tomorrow we will do something exciting together, that I promise you."

She dropped a kiss on Prunella's cheek, who asked:

"Surely somebody is calling for you?"

"Yes, of course," Nanette answered, "but Godmama said they would wait downstairs, and I am late as it is."

She hurried from the room before Prunella could formulate any other questions.

Then with a little sigh she rose from the chair on which she had been sitting and walked to the table on which there was a vase of flowers.

They made her think of home, and there was an ache in her heart when she thought of the flowers in the garden, the green lawns sloping down to a small stream, and her horse waiting for her in the stables.

'That is where I want to be,' she thought.

She found herself wondering whether the Earl was riding every morning on the gallop and if she would ever own a horse swift enough to beat Caesar.

It seemed absurd, in fact she told herself it was sheer imagination, but she missed the Earl, her fights with him, and even the feeling of disapproval which he aroused in her whenever they met.

What was he doing now? How many paintings had he sold? When she went back, would there be nothing left in the Gallery?

It was agonising to think of what had been lost, and yet instead of seeing the treasures she loved she had a different vision in her mind.

It was of the Earl himself, the mocking look in his eyes, the twist to his lips, the manner in which he was entirely at his ease in his untidy, rather disreputable clothes.

Wherever he was, he seemed to dominate everything, even the Gold Salon and herself.

'I hate him!' she thought.

At the same time, she wanted to see him. She wanted to spar with him, to hear his deep voice, to try to get the better of him in an argument.

"He is destroying everything I love, everything I have cared for," she told herself.

Then she had the uncomfortable feeling that it was more pleasant to be with him, and to be shocked and angry, than to be alone as she was now in a dismal Hotel in a city she disliked.

Prunella wondered why anyone found London alluring.

It might be all right for Nanette, surrounded

as she was by young people, but to Prunella the streets were narrow and dirty, and she missed the freshness of the air, and the horses she could ride at home.

Most of all she missed everything that was familiar at home and in which she was personally involved.

She knew now how much she enjoyed owning the Manor, having people in the village turning to her for advice and help, and, most of all, looking after the Winslow Estate and the Hall.

Last year, after her father had died, there had hardly been a day when she had not gone to the great house to see if there was anything that needed doing.

Most of all, to wander through it, enjoying the beauty of the Salons, the ceilings, the paintings, the State-Rooms, and to know with a feeling of pride that she had prevented many of them from deteriorating or suffering irreparable damage through neglect.

"I want to go home," she said suddenly beneath her breath, but she was thinking of the Hall, not the Manor.

To her dismay, she was suddenly aware that there were tears in her eyes, and even as she tried to blink them away, ashamed at her own weakness, the door opened and a servant announced:

"A gentleman to see you, Miss."

Prunella looked up through her tears, but for a moment she was not certain that it was the Earl.

He looked so different, but it did not immediately strike her what the difference was, until she realised that he was wearing evening-dress, which was very different in every way from what he had worn when she and Nanette had dined with him at the Hall.

Now his long-tailed coat, with its silk revers, fitted as if it were a second skin, his cravat was as intricately tied in a complicated style as anything she had seen on his nephew, and the points of his collar reached above his sunburnt chin at exactly the right angle.

"Good-evening, Prunella!"

After a little hesitation from sheer surprise, Prunella remembered to curtsey.

"Good-evening . . . My Lord."

"I see you are alone. I was half-afraid you would either be at some amusing party or entertaining."

"Nanette is dining with her Godmother, Lady Carnworth."

"And you were not invited?"

"Her Ladyship was kind enough to have me to dinner three nights ago."

"So tonight Cinderella is left at home. Well, I am prepared to offer you an evening that will be more interesting than moping here."

"That is very kind of Your Lordship . . . but I am quite . . . happy, thank . . . you."

"I think that is untrue," the Earl said, "and, as you are so hospitable, I would enjoy a glass of sherry."

Prunella gave a little start.

"I am sorry," she said, "I should have offered you some refreshment, but I was in fact so surprised to see you."

"You were thinking of me as being at the Hall?" the Earl enquired.

"Yes, of course! I thought you would have too much to do to wish to come to London."

"I found my work considerably impeded because you were not there to help me."

He noticed that for a moment there was a glint in Prunella's eyes before she replied:

"I doubt that is . . . true."

"But I assure you I am speaking the truth. I missed you, Prunella, and I am perceptive enough to think you missed me — or rather my house."

Prunella turned away and rang the bell, and before it was answered she seated herself in a chair and with her hand indicated one near it.

"Will you not sit down, My Lord?"

"Thank you."

As she leant back and crossed her legs, she thought that he seemed very relaxed, while she felt tense and, for no reason she could understand, a little nervous.

A servant answered the bell, and she ordered sherry for the Earl and a glass of Madeira for herself.

"Are you brave enough to defy the conventions and have supper with me?" the Earl asked.

"Would that not be . . . wrong?" Prunella enquired.

He realised that she really did not know the

answer, and he said:

"Not exactly wrong, though perhaps a little indiscreet. Unfortunately, as I know no-one I can ask to join us at this late hour in the evening, I suggest we go first to the Theatre Royal, Drury Lane, where I have already ordered a Box, then to some quiet, discreet place for supper, where we can talk."

It sounded to Prunella so exciting, after the dull evening she had expected for herself, that she wanted to answer that there was nothing she would enjoy more.

Instead she said in a prim little voice:

"It is very kind of Your Lordship to think of me when there must be so many old friends longing to see you, since your return to England after being away for so . . . long."

"Are you gunning for me, Prunella?"

"No, of course not!"

"I can hear that little sting in your voice when you refer to my long absence abroad, and I am tired of excusing myself by pointing out that there was a war taking place, or perhaps it would be better to be honest and say I had rather more important things to do than crawl humbly home and be, as Pascoe has suggested, the 'Prodigal Son.' "

"At least he had the fatted calf killed for him," Prunella said, without really considering her words.

Then she wished she had not spoken, as the Earl laughed.

"You are quite right, Prunella, there was no-one to kill a calf, fatted or otherwise, except yourself."

There was silence, then Prunella said:

"I do not mean, My Lord, to sound as if I am continually . . . reproaching you. We promised to help each other, but I am not certain you are keeping to your part of the bargain."

"Only time will tell you that," the Earl replied, and Prunella was not certain what he meant.

She noticed when the sherry arrived that the Earl took only a sip from his glass, and she had the feeling that he had asked for it merely to put her in the wrong by making her appear inhospitable.

At the same time, she had no wish to quarrel, and despite her conviction that she ought to refuse his invitation, she went eagerly to her bedroom to collect a wrap to wear over her green gown.

Nanette had fortunately been most insistent that every evening-gown should have a scarf to match it, and a number of them were trimmed with maribou or fur.

It was a warm night and Prunella's long scarf was of soft chiffon, which she wrapped round her. Although she was not aware of it, it made her look like the embodiment of spring just coming into bud.

She took a swift glance at herself in the mirror, seeing that the new style in which her hair was dressed was neat and becoming. Then, with an irrepressible light in her eyes and a smile on her lips, she joined the Earl in the Sitting-Room.

Outside the Hotel, Prunella found that the Earl had waiting for him a very smart closed carriage drawn by two horses.

There was a coachman and a footman on the box and she supposed that he had hired them and wondered what it must have cost.

The carriage she and Nanette had hired while they were in London was drawn by only one horse and had only one coachman, but it had still seemed to Prunella to be extremely expensive.

As they drove along Piccadilly she found herself remembering excitedly that the Theatre Royal, Drury Lane, which had been burnt down for the second time in 1809, had been rebuilt three years later.

She had read about it in the newspapers and had been so interested because her father had met and often talked about Samuel Whitbread, who had raised four hundred thousand pounds for the rebuilding of the Theatre.

Prunella had read that it was magnificent and she knew it was something she wished to see, and, what was even more exciting this year, the *Morning Post* had told her that they had installed gas in the Theatre as an illuminant.

She was so deep in her thoughts as to what lay ahead that she felt quite surprised when the Earl, sitting beside her, asked:

"What are you thinking about? One thing is

quite obvious — it is not your host!"

Prunella blushed.

"I am sorry," she said. "Am I being rude? I was thinking about the Theatre Royal and how exciting it will be to see it. Will Edmund Kean be playing tonight?"

"He will," the Earl answered, "and after everything that has been said about him as the greatest actor of our time, I think you would like to see him play Othello."

He knew by the way Prunella drew in her breath and clasped her hands together that she was excited, and when they sat in the Box in what was undoubtedly the finest Theatre London had ever seen, the look in her eyes was that of a child seeing a lighted Christmas-tree for the first time.

Edmund Kean was born to smoulder, to glow, and to blaze with such an intensity of glory that he consumed himself in the white-hot fire of his genius.

When he had first elected to play Othello, the prophets of gloom had forecast failure.

But his dramatic prowess knew no bounds and his Othello was acclaimed as the most perfect of all the portrayals of the Moor of Venice. Kean surpassed all he had done before, and Lord Byron had cried:

"By God, he is a soul!"

To Prunella, *Othello* was a revelation and she felt herself carried away by Kean's brilliant acting and by the magic of the Theatre itself.

She had never had an opportunity of visiting a Play-House since she was grown up and had seen only performances given by amateurs in the nearest town to Little Stodbury.

Now she felt as if she herself were part of Shakespeare's drama. She suffered the agonies of Desdemona and the wild grief of Othello until their tragedy was hers and she had been transported out of herself.

Only as the curtain finally fell did she come back to the real world from the magical one where she had been emotionally moved in a manner which she had never experienced in her whole life.

She had not been aware that while she was watching the stage, the Earl had been watching her and understanding what she was feeling.

Somehow it was impossible to utter commonplaces or even to thank him for an unforgettable experience. She could only move in silence through the Theatre to where the Earl's carriage was waiting outside.

Only as they drove away did Prunella say in a very small voice:

"I did not . . . know I could . . . feel like that."

There was no need to explain what she meant, and the Earl said quietly:

"I knew that you could, but I wanted to have evidence of it."

She was too bemused to ask him for an explanation, and only when she found herself sitting in a small Restaurant not far from the Theatre

Royal did she say, as the Earl asked her what she would like:

"I feel as if I . . . could never eat . . . or drink again."

"You will," the Earl replied with confidence. "I am therefore going to order what I think you will enjoy."

Prunella had no wish to argue with him, and when the waiter poured out a glass of champagne she sipped it absently, her ears still seeming to hear Kean's vibrant voice.

Then when the food came, she found, surprisingly, that she was hungry, and after she had eaten a few mouthfuls she gave a little laugh and said to the Earl:

"Forgive me, but I have never known anything so . . . moving and in a way so . . . marvellous!"

He did not reply, and she added:

"I told you I was a country mouse."

"I am actually congratulating myself," he said, "in having taken you to see something which I knew, unless I was a bad judge of character, would move you as the story of Othello has always moved me."

"It is very sad."

"Like all women, you would like a love-story to end happily."

"How could he not have realised that she . . . loved him?"

"Do you feel, after that, that you now know a little more about love than you knew previously?" the Earl enquired.

The way he spoke made Prunella look at him quickly. Then she said:

"I think perhaps . . . one has to . . . be in love . . . oneself, to know . . . anything about it."

"And you have never been in love?"

"No . . . of course not!"

"Why so vehement? If there were any justice in the world you should have been in love a dozen times already at your age."

Unexpectedly Prunella found herself thinking of the man her mother had run away with.

That had not been love, not real love, and yet she knew there had been a reflection of it in that he had meant something in her mother's life, and when he betrayed her something precious had been shattered.

"Who was he, Prunella?" the Earl asked.

The question startled her and she looked at him, then looked away again.

"There was . . . no-one."

"That is not true! For a moment I could see you living again what you felt, and suffered."

"You are talking nonsense," she said quickly.

"On the contrary, you are denying the truth, which I always find rather tiresome, and yet it is the inevitable habit of most women."

"I always tell the truth!" Prunella asserted angrily.

"Then tell me whom you loved and what happened."

Almost as if he compelled her, she said:

"It was . . . not like . . . that . . . I just . . . ad-

140

mired someone . . . and because he said charming . . . and flattering things to me . . . I found myself . . . thinking about him . . . and perhaps . . . d-dreaming of him too. . . ."

She stopped speaking and the Earl said quietly:

"Then you were disillusioned? In what way?"

"I have . . . no wish to . . . explain what . . . h-happened . . . but I . . . s-suppose it made me feel suspicious of men and everything . . . they . . . do."

"It is time you grew up, Prunella," the Earl said. "That was a childish dream and children are often disappointed. Now that you are older, you will have to realise that no-one is perfect, any more than you are yourself."

She looked at him without speaking, and he went on:

"If you think that women are unsure and uncertain of themselves, men are too. They do valiant deeds to pretend they are braver than they really are. They even attempt the impossible, to satisfy some imperfection in themselves."

"I did not . . . think of . . . men as ever feeling like . . . that," Prunella said.

"I think you thought they were all strong, omnipotent, imperious, as a child believes her father to be," the Earl smiled, "but you will find they are weak, sometimes afraid, and very much in need of tenderness."

The way he spoke was so astonishing that Prunella stared at him wide-eyed, and he said:

"Think back and you will find I am right. Your

father was a dominating man, as mine was, and I fought wildly, frantically, against being made subservient, against being manipulated and forced to obey orders that were given to me without explanation."

There was that twisted smile on his lips that was somehow very intriguing as he went on:

"Now I am beginning to realise that my father was just a man who in many ways was disappointed with life and who, to placate his own conscience, wished to appear the conquering hero he never was in reality."

"I never thought that he, or Papa, was like that," Prunella said.

Then she began to wonder if the Earl was not right.

His father had, in his subtle way, always tried to prove he was right, and he directed and even dominated the lives of all those round him.

The Earl watched the expression on her face and after a little while he said:

"I see you begin to understand. Now think about yourself and your own reactions."

Being taken off her guard, Prunella had a sudden vision of her mother, very beautiful with her fair hair and blue eyes, laughing as she played in the sunshine with Nanette and herself.

Then, as she chased them between the trees and over the grass towards the lily-pool, her father had unexpectedly appeared walking towards them, leaning on his cane.

Prunella could remember all too clearly now

how there had seemed to be a sudden silence as she and her mother had stopped running, while Nanette, who could barely toddle, sat down on the grass.

Her mother had walked towards her father.

"I was playing with the children," she said, her voice a little breathless, her hands trying to tidy her hair.

"So I see," Sir Roderick had remarked briefly. "I want you, Lucia. Kindly come back to the house with me."

"Yes, of course, Roderick."

Her mother's voice had been meek and she had turned to Prunella.

"Run to Charity, dearest," she had said, "and take Nanette with you."

"But, Mama, you promised to play with us," Prunella protested.

"Your father wants me, darling. I will come and see you later in the Nursery."

Her mother had gone walking sedately beside her father, who was very slow.

Because that moment of time had come back so vividly, Prunella said almost angrily to the Earl:

"We are being introspective and what is the point of it? It cannot undo what has happened."

"Of course not," he answered, "but what we can avoid is allowing it to remain in the shadows of the past instead of leaving it behind to come out into the sunshine."

"Is that what you are asking me to do?"

"Yes," the Earl said, "and with me, Prunella!"

Her eyes widened.

She looked at him for an explanation and the expression she saw in his eyes made her stiffen.

She did not know why, but she felt her heart beating strangely in her breast and a feeling she did not understand crept over her.

It was what she felt when she listened to Edmund Kean as Othello making love, and yet because it was within herself it was more intense.

"I do not . . . understand . . . what you are . . . s-saying," she faltered.

"I think you do," the Earl said quietly. "You see, Prunella, I have been looking for you for a very long time."

"I . . . I do not . . . understand."

Prunella forced her eyes away from his, and now she was staring across the room, conscious as she did so that although he had not moved, the Earl was somehow closer to her and she was acutely conscious of him.

He was overwhelming and overpowering and she wanted to run away and yet she wanted to stay.

Then as if from far away she saw two people come into the Restaurant.

The waiter was leading them to a secluded table and as they followed him there was no mistaking who they were.

It was Nanette and with her was Pascoe!

Chapter Six

"How could she? How could she lie to me?" Prunella said over and over again as they drove from the Restaurant back towards the Hotel.

Nanette and Pascoe had not been aware that she and the Earl were in the same Restaurant and had seen them, and although in her first fury at having been deceived Prunella had wished to go and confront them, the Earl had prevented her.

She had half-risen to her feet when she felt his hand on her wrist.

"No!" he said firmly. "You cannot make a scene here!"

"I only want her to know I have seen her and am aware of her lies and deception," Prunella replied.

"And what good will that do?"

Because the Earl's hand held her prisoner and she felt him drawing her back into her seat, she sat down again.

"I trusted her when she said she was going out with her Godmother," Prunella said almost as if she spoke to herself, "and I suppose on all the other evenings when I thought I was not invited with her, she was in fact with your nephew."

"Is that so very reprehensible when she has seen him so many times before?" the Earl enquired.

"She . . . lied to . . . me."

"I imagine she did so because she knew the fuss you would make if she wished to see the man she loves and who loves her."

"Are you condoning their behaviour?" Prunella asked incredulously.

"Not condoning it," the Earl replied, "but trying to understand why Nanette has behaved as she has. You are a very formidable person, Prunella, when you are being aggressive."

She looked at him and he saw a sudden bewilderment in her eyes, as if she had not expected him to attack her.

"I do not . . . mean to be," she said after a moment. "I am only trying to do what is . . . right."

"What is right for one person is not necessarily right for another, and who can decide what is right or wrong where love is concerned?"

"I do not believe Nanette is really in love with your nephew," Prunella said sharply. "She is too young to know anything about real love, which lasts for a lifetime."

"While you, of course, know a great deal about it," the Earl said mockingly.

Prunella did not answer but he saw her lips tighten, and after a moment he said:

"Stop being so unnecessarily upset. I assure you, although it is perhaps reprehensible of

Nanette to have supper alone with Pascoe, she will come to no harm. He loves her."

As if Prunella understood the meaning behind the words, he saw the colour rise in her cheeks, and after a moment she said a little incoherently:

"I was . . . not thinking . . . of anything like . . . that."

"I thought, from the way you were behaving, that that was in your mind."

"No, of course not!" she said in a shocked voice. "But I am very annoyed and hurt that Nanette should lie to me so . . . blatantly."

"I can understand that," the Earl said, "but you have to learn, Prunella, that when one is in love, nobody else, not even one's nearest and dearest, has any importance beside the man or the woman who has captured one's heart."

"What am I to do?" Prunella asked desperately. "How can I stop Nanette from seeing your nephew and endangering her reputation by having supper in public with him?"

"If you really think her reputation will be ruined, what about your own?"

Again the colour rose in Prunella's cheeks, but she answered:

"I am older and completely unknown in London, and you are . . . different."

"In what way?"

Prunella had not expected the question and she found it hard to find an answer.

In fact, as she tried in her confusion to find words, he said mockingly:

"Perhaps you are accusing me also of being a fortune-hunter?"

"No, of course not," Prunella said quickly.

"Are you sure? After all, even if you are not as rich as your sister, you still own the Manor and its grounds and have a considerable income, much of which has already been expended on my property."

"I do not wish to . . . talk about myself," Prunella said after a moment's hesitation, "but you promised me you would try to help me to prevent your nephew from paying so much attention to Nanette. Instead of which, I think you have made the situation worse."

"I asked him to stay with me so that I could judge for myself if the things you told me about him are true."

"And now you know they are?"

"I believe he is not the danger you consider him to be."

"Of course he is a danger!" Prunella said crossly. "He is trying to marry Nanette and she is infatuated with him! And how can she help it, when he is so good-looking and has what Charity calls 'a honeyed tongue'?"

She did not mean to be funny but when the Earl laughed a faint smile touched the corners of her lips.

"It is exactly what he has," she said helplessly, "and of course Nanette is mesmerised by him like a stupid little rabbit."

"I think your metaphors are a little mixed,"

the Earl said. "At the same time, I know what you are saying and I too find my nephew has 'a honeyed tongue.' "

"He pulled the wool over your eyes, and you still believe he loves Nanette and not her money?"

"I think it would be difficult for anyone, even you, Prunella, to blind me to the truth," the Earl said, "and the truth is, whether you like it or not, Pascoe loves your sister as much as he is capable of loving anybody, and I think she feels the same about him."

"If that is what you feel, then there is nothing more for me to say on the subject," Prunella said stiffly, "and I would like to go home."

"Of course," the Earl agreed.

He called for the bill and when it was paid he rose to his feet and said to Prunella:

"I want you to leave without attracting your sister's attention."

The Earl thought she was about to argue with him, but instead she gave a little toss of her head and, pulling her chiffon scarf round her shoulders, walked straight out of the Restaurant, looking neither to right nor to left.

The Earl followed her and when they had stepped into his carriage, which was waiting outside, they drove for some way in silence until, as if she knew she was being rude, Prunella said:

"I must thank Your Lordship for taking me to *Othello*. I enjoyed it more than I can say, and my evening was only spoilt by . . . what happened . . . afterwards."

"I should have thought the play might have taught you, if nothing else, that it is a mistake to jump to hasty conclusions."

"You can hardly compare what Othello thought about Desdemona with what I feel about your nephew."

"I think if you look for it you will find a similarity," the Earl said drily.

Prunella thought he was being rather stupid in his defence of both Pascoe's and Nanette's behaviour and she planned in her mind exactly what she was going to say to her sister.

Nanette was ignorant of the fact that she had been seen, her deception discovered, and her lies exposed.

Because Prunella loved Nanette it was an agony to think she had lied to her not once but probably several times since they came to London.

Where had she been on Wednesday night when she had said she was dining with some friends she had met on her previous visit?

And Prunella remembered another day when she had said she had been asked out to luncheon and she had looked very pretty, in fact radiant, before she left the Hotel.

Of course she had been going to meet Pascoe, but why had she not told her the truth?

Prunella knew the answer to that question, but she kept telling herself that if she had been told, she would have been reasonable about it and would even have acquiesced and allowed her sister to meet Pascoe Lowes.

She thought now that she had been very foolish in not realising that if he was in London it was obvious that he would call to see Nanette at the Hotel, if he had not been meeting her elsewhere.

'I should have suspected they were doing something behind my back,' Prunella thought bitterly, and was surprised to find that they had arrived at the Hotel.

Deep in her thoughts, she stepped out and went up the stairs towards her Suite, hardly aware that the Earl was accompanying her.

They went into the Sitting-Room, which still looked gloomy even though it was lit by candles in the sconces on the walls and a small brass chandelier hanging from the ceiling.

Prunella, still resenting how she had been treated by Nanette, threw her gloves and her scarf down on a chair, then walked towards the fireplace to turn as she reached it and say to the Earl:

"You have to help me! I will talk to Nanette, but you must speak to your nephew."

"What about?"

"Leaving Nanette alone. We could suggest that they do not see each other for a year, in which case I could have the chance, as I intended when I came to London, to find her a new interest."

"What you mean is another man," the Earl said. "Do you really believe she could fall out of love so quickly or that you, even with your extensive acquaintance with presentable young men, could find someone as handsome as Pascoe?"

He was being sarcastic and mocking her, but Prunella was past caring.

"You have to help me, you have to!" she insisted. "I will not allow my sister to make a disastrous marriage just because she has money."

"Are you quite certain it would be disastrous?"

"Of course I am certain!" Prunella snapped. "Your nephew has chased after a number of heiresses who have managed to elude his greedy, grasping hands, and, as I have said until I am tired of saying it, it is only because Nanette is so young that she cannot see what he is really like beneath his dandified appearance."

"You are very vehement, Prunella," the Earl said, "but what I find so pathetic is that you are railing against something that is bigger than yourself."

She looked at him questioningly and he said quietly:

"Love! Something about which you, Prunella, know nothing, and which is, as I have told you once before, irresistible and, as we saw tonight at the Theatre, overwhelming and uncontrollable."

"What is depicted on a stage is very different from real life."

"How do you know?"

"Of course it is," she argued. "What we were watching was very skilfully portrayed, but by cardboard characters. They suffered agonies because of their emotions, but that sort of thing does not happen in real life."

"How do you know that?"

"Because it does not."

"If you had ever been in love, Prunella, you would know that your body becomes a battleground of conflicting sensations, and love can carry you high into a rapturous Heaven or cast you into the darkest depths of Hell."

Prunella gave a little laugh that had no humour in it.

"Now you are being dramatic," she said, "and not as skilfully as Edmund Kean!"

"I think, Prunella," the Earl said slowly, "you are offering me a challenge to make you feel dramatic too."

"A . . . challenge?"

She looked at the Earl as she spoke and realised he was standing very close to her.

Because she had been concentrating on Nanette, she had not really looked at him since they had left the Restaurant, and in the Theatre she had been intent on watching the play.

Now she realised how different he looked in his new clothes, and how, in a way, magnificent.

He was not as handsome as his nephew, but he had, as Nanette had seen the first time she met him, the raffish look of a pirate or a buccaneer, which was in fact very noticeable at the moment.

His eyes seemed dark and penetrating as they looked into hers, and because they were standing close to each other Prunella was suddenly very conscious of how tall and broad-shouldered he was, and how very masculine.

She had never been close to an attractive man in the same way before, and it gave her a strange feeling which she could not understand and which she instinctively thought she should avoid.

She would have taken a step backwards but the mantelpiece behind her prevented her from doing so, and she could only stand with her eyes held by the Earl's and feel that for the moment everything she had been saying was swept away from her mind and there was no other problem except him.

"I wanted you, Prunella, to come to London," he said, "and broaden your horizons. But I suppose it is too soon to know if London by itself can do this for you, so perhaps we should find a different way of achieving the same thing."

"I do not . . . know what you are . . . talking about."

"I am talking about love," the Earl said, "and of course your ignorance of it."

"I am not ashamed of being ignorant, My Lord, if love makes people behave in a deceitful, underhanded manner."

"And how would you behave in the same circumstances?"

"I would always do what is right."

The Earl laughed softly.

"You are so very positive and still so aggressive, and yet I find it attractive because you are so different from anyone I have ever met before."

"By that I understand you to mean that you have met some very . . . strange people."

"Of course they have been that, but they were none of them as lovely as you, Prunella, or as prudish."

He had not appeared to move, and yet Prunella had the uncomfortable feeling that he was nearer to her than he had been a moment earlier.

"I think, My Lord . . ." she began.

Then to her astonishment the Earl's arms were round her, he pulled her against him, and his lips were on hers.

For a moment she was too surprised to do anything but freeze into immobility.

Then as she began to struggle, his arms tightened and his lips against hers were demanding.

She felt that he held her completely captive, and as he held her close against him, his mouth made her his prisoner in a way that she had never imagined was possible through a kiss.

Even as she told herself that what he was doing was outrageous and she hated him for it, she felt a strange sensation she had never known before rise within her, move through her body, up to her throat, and into her lips.

It was like a warm wave flowing relentlessly

through her and at the same time filling her mind with a radiance and a light that seemed to shine from her heart.

It was so strange, so utterly inexpressible, and yet in a way it was so wonderful that, despite herself, she felt her resistance cease as she surrendered her lips and her whole body to what he asked of her.

She knew that his mouth was fierce and demanding, passionate and insistent, and yet when it should have disgusted and frightened her, she found instead that she was subservient to his demands.

Then when she felt as if time and place had ceased to exist, that her feet were no longer on the ground, and that he was carrying her up into a cloudless sky, he twisted her lips with his.

The sudden pain was so intense that it was almost like lightning streaking through her, to be succeeded by a feeling of rapture and wonder that was indescribable.

She only knew that for the moment she felt as if she had touched the stars and held them to her breast.

Then when the ecstasy of it was almost too intense to bear, the Earl raised his head.

Because for the moment Prunella could think of nothing but what he had made her feel, she gave a little murmur that came from the depths of her heart and hid her face against his shoulder.

He did not speak but only held her closer with

a strength which made her feel as if he prevented her from falling, and his lips were against her hair.

How long they stood there Prunella could afterwards never remember.

She only knew that her whole being was struggling with the feelings he had aroused in her.

She felt as if her heart were singing; her eyes were still blinded by a light that came from themselves or perhaps from the stars to which they had journeyed.

Then as she tried to come back to earth she heard the Earl say:

"Now do you understand, my sweet, what I have been saying to you?"

He kissed her forehead before he went on:

"How soon will you marry me so that I can continue to teach you about love?"

Prunella drew in her breath.

For a moment she thought she could not have heard what he had said and must have imagined it.

Then, with what was almost a superhuman effort, because she needed the strength of his arms to hold her, she forced herself away from him.

"What . . . did you . . . say?" she asked in a very small voice.

"I asked you to marry me," he replied. "After all, if you think about it, my darling, what could be more suitable? You have already made the Hall part of yourself."

"D-do you really . . . think I would . . . marry you?" Prunella enquired.

"Can you think of any reason why you should not do so?" the Earl asked.

He did not move but she put out her hands as if she felt he was encroaching on her.

"Of course I could not . . . do such . . . a thing!"

"Why not?"

"How could I do anything that would give Nanette grounds for thinking I must approve of the way in which she is . . . behaving?"

"I am not concerned with Nanette," the Earl replied, "but with us — you and me, Prunella. Although you may not agree with me at the moment, we would be very happy together."

As if she thought her legs were too weak to carry her, Prunella sat down in a chair.

"Please," she pleaded. "I cannot . . . talk about this . . . now."

The Earl stood looking at her and he knew she had no idea how lovely she looked in her green gown with her eyes wide and still a little ecstatic from the emotions he had aroused in her, a flush on her cheeks, her lips red and soft from his lips.

"We will talk about it tomorrow," he said quietly. "Go to bed and dream of what I made you feel just now."

He moved to her side, took her hand, and raised it to his lips.

He kissed the back of it and then turned it over

to kiss the softness of her palm.

He felt a little quiver go through her, and as her eyes met his he said quietly in his deep voice:

"I love you! Do not worry about anything else, just remember what this was like."

He released her hand and walked to the door without looking back, and when he had gone Prunella gave a little cry and put her hands up to her face.

It was dawn before Prunella fell asleep, and when she awoke it was far later than her usual time of being awakened and she knew that Charity had let her sleep.

Everything she had thought and felt the night before came flooding over her and once again she told herself, as she had done in the hours of darkness, that what had happened to her with the Earl was inconceivable, incredible, and must have been part of her imagination!

And yet it actually had happened.

He had kissed her and aroused in her feelings which she had no idea existed and which she had to admit were wonderful and beyond the bounds of her imagination.

It was, she told herself, something which must never occur again, and that the Earl had asked her to marry him was too amazing to be credible.

He had known what she felt about him before they came to London!

He had known that she was shocked by his behaviour in the past and by his staying away from home for fourteen years, and if he was not aware that she despised him for selling the Van Dykes, then he must be far more obtuse than he appeared to be.

No, he knew, and perhaps he had deliberately defied her because she had asked him not to sell them.

But all this which concerned only herself was immaterial compared with the fact that if she married the Earl, then there would be no possibility of her preventing Nanette from throwing herself away on his fortune-hunting nephew and ruining her life for all time.

"I must not see him again," Prunella told herself, and wondered how she could ever prevent herself from remembering what he had made her feel.

It has been an ecstasy that was not of this world, and instinctively she tried to arm herself against the feelings he had aroused in her.

"I will have to leave with Nanette," she whispered to herself in the darkness, and wondered why it was difficult to speak with lips that had been kissed.

Now with a dull light coming through the sides of the curtains she told herself that she had to be strong.

First she would remonstrate with Nanette for her behaviour of last night and for the lies she had told her, and then she must think of some way by which she could not only prevent Nanette from seeing Pascoe but prevent herself from seeing the Earl.

There was no time to lose and she got quickly out of bed. Putting on a very attractive robe which Nanette had made her buy, of heavy silk trimmed with lace and velvet ribbons, she crossed the room to pull back the curtains.

It was raining outside and she thought the grey sky was symbolic of the task which lay ahead of her.

She combed her hair, put on her bedroom slippers, and went into Nanette's room.

Her sister was sitting up in bed, finishing her breakfast, which had been brought to her on a tray.

"Good-morning, Prunella!" she said. "Charity told me that you were not awake. It is unlike you to sleep so late. You are not ill?"

"I am not ill," Prunella replied, "but upset."

Nanette raised her eye-brows and Prunella asked:

"Where were you last night . . . and with whom?"

"I told you . . ." Nanette began; then she saw the expression on her sister's face and exclaimed: "Oh — you know!"

"I saw you!"

"Saw me? How?"

"I happened to be having supper in the same Restaurant as you were."

"Good Heavens!" Nanette exclaimed. "I did not see you. Whom were you with?"

"I was with the Earl, and I could hardly believe

my eyes, Nanette, when I saw you come in with his nephew and realised how you had deceived me and lied to me."

"I am sorry — dearest," Nanette said lightly, "but you know what a fuss you would have made if I had told you I was going out with Pascoe, and I *had* to see him! Besides, I have had enough of those dreary dinner-parties with our boring relations and even listening to Godmama gossipping always in the same way about the same people. Her conversation never varies."

"What we were talking about," Prunella said scathingly, "is your behaviour in deceiving me."

"I know you are angry," Nanette answered, "but do try to understand, Prunella, that I love Pascoe and I intend to marry him."

"Over my dead body!" Prunella said firmly. "Let me make this clear once and for all, Nanette. You will not marry Pascoe, or if you do, it will not be until you are twenty-one, which means you will have to wait three years."

She saw her sister go very pale and she went on:

"I very much doubt if *he* will wait for you as long as that, for there will doubtless be other heiresses for him to chase long before you are available."

"How can you be so — cruel and so — unkind to — me?" Nanette asked.

"Although you will not believe it, I am thinking entirely of your happiness," Prunella said. "Both Pascoe and his uncle are ne'er-dowells and I intend that we shall have nothing more to do with either of them."

"How do you propose to manage that?" Nanette asked scornfully. "How can you avoid seeing the Earl when he lives next door, or Pascoe, if he is staying with him?"

"We will avoid them because we are not going home!"

"Not going home?" Nanette exclaimed.

"No. I have made up my mind," Prunella replied. "I am taking you to Bath, where quite a number of people go at this time of the year, so there is a good chance you will meet a man there who will prove much more suitable as a husband than the one you have chosen for yourself."

"That is impossible!" Nanette cried, but Prunella continued as if she had not spoken:

"If Bath proves disappointing, then we might consider going to France . . . to Paris."

Nanette looked at her sister incredulously.

"I think you have gone mad!" she said. "Why should you drag me round the world simply because you think I will forget Pascoe? I shall never forget him! Never! I love him, and I intend to marry him whatever you may say or do."

"A great deal can happen in three years," Prunella said.

Feeling that there was nothing more to say, she walked out of Nanette's bedroom, closing the door sharply behind her.

When she was dressed she sent Charity downstairs to ask the Manager of the Hotel to come and speak to her in the Sitting-Room.

When he arrived he bowed politely at the door as Prunella said:

"I wish to talk to you, Mr. Mayhew."

"I'm honoured, Miss Broughton," the Manager replied. "I'm only hoping you've not any complaints to make as to the comfort of your rooms or the service you've received."

"No, indeed, Mr. Mayhew, you have done everything possible for me and my sister," Prunella answered. "What I want you to arrange is a Courier and a conveyance to take us to Bath."

"To Bath, Miss Broughton?" Mr. Mayhew exclaimed in surprise.

"We have decided to go there for a short visit," Prunella said. "I have had no chance to make arrangements, and I want your Courier to take us to a quiet, respectable Hotel and see that we have the same accommodation that we have had here."

"Of course, Miss Broughton. It'll be a great pleasure to make this arrangement for you."

Mr. Mayhew paused for a moment before he said:

"I hope it'll be possible to find a Courier who is suitable and of course a carriage and horses at such short notice. But I'll try to perform miracles, and I hope that you and Miss Nanette Broughton will be able to leave here at perhaps ten o'clock tomorrow morning."

"Thank you very much, Mr. Mayhew," Prunella said briskly. "It is extremely obliging of you, and I know if my father were alive he would thank you for the care you have taken of us."

"I'm deeply touched by the kind things you say," Mr. Mayhew replied.

Then he bowed himself from the room and Prunella went in search of Charity, whom she found in her bedroom.

As she told the old woman what she was about to do, Charity threw up her hands in dismay.

"Mercy on us, Miss Prunella!" she exclaimed. "What's come over you? This rush, rush, tear, tear — leaves me not knowing if I'm standing on my head or my heels. Bath indeed! What's wrong with going home?"

"You know the answer to that," Prunella replied crossly. "Miss Nanette will see Mr. Lowes, and that is something I am determined to prevent."

She thought Charity was going to argue with her, but instead she went away muttering beneath her breath, and Prunella went to the wardrobe to find one of her new bonnets and to search for her gloves and sunshade.

Some of her new gowns had not yet been delivered, and she knew that she must have them sent today if they were to travel with her tomorrow.

She thought that by this time Nanette would be dressed, and she went into her room to find that only Charity was there.

"Where is Miss Nanette?" she asked.

"She's downstairs."

Prunella's lips tightened.

"That means she is sending a note to Mr. Lowes," she said. "Why did you not stop her, Charity? You know it is something I will not allow!"

"Miss Nanette's grown up," Charity replied, "and there's no use, Miss Prunella, treating her as if she were a child. She's a will of her own, and if you drive her too hard you'll regret it."

"Do not be so ridiculous, Charity!" Prunella snapped. "Miss Nanette is behaving extremely badly and that is something I will not tolerate."

At the same time, she wondered, with a little sinking of her heart, what she would do if now that Pascoe knew where they were going he followed them to Bath. In that case, they would have run away for nothing.

Then she had a clever idea and wondered why she had not thought of it before.

She had told Nanette and Charity, and the Hotel Manager, for that matter, that they were going to Bath.

At the last moment she would change her plans and instead of Bath they would go to Cheltenham.

She had read in the newspapers that at this time of the year a great number of people congregated in Cheltenham both for the races and to drink the waters of the Spa.

But that was not to say that the visitors were mostly invalids, and, if the newspapers were to be believed, the Balls in the Assembly-Rooms which the Duke of Wellington himself had attended and the Theatre Royal where Mrs. Siddons had performed were equal to anything to be seen in London.

'We will go to Cheltenham,' Prunella thought with a little smile of triumph, 'and it will be a very long time before Pascoe finds out where we have gone, especially if I manage to prevent any of Nanette's letters from reaching him.'

The Earl had talked of a challenge. Very well, Prunella thought, this was a challenge in which she would prove the victor.

Just for a moment she found herself remembering the wonder and rapture of his kiss and the strange sensations he had given her which she still thought were not of this world.

Then she told herself firmly that what she felt or did not feel was of no importance in relation to her duty, which was to save Nanette.

Very well, she would save her sister without the Earl's help, and she had the feeling that Cheltenham would solve her problems because the idea had come to her almost like an inspiration.

"I will show the Earl I am cleverer than he is," Prunella murmured.

Then she found herself wondering how many of the Van Dykes he had sold to pay for his new clothes in which he looked so magnificent.

Prunella and Nanette had been invited to luncheon by an elderly Judge who had been a friend of their father.

Prunella had remembered his name and had written, when they first arrived in London, to ask Sir Simeon Hunt if he would call on them at their Hotel.

He had replied, as she had expected, that he would be delighted to entertain them at his house in Park Street.

Although Nanette was pale and rather silent, she did not make any comment when Prunella had returned to the Hotel after visiting several shops in Bond Street.

"I am afraid, dearest, you will not remember Sir Simeon Hunt," Prunella said as they drove towards Park Street, "but he was a very distinguished-looking man when I last saw him, and Papa always said he had one of the finest brains there had ever been at the Bar."

"How interesting!" Nanette remarked in a tone that implied that as far as she was concerned it was nothing of the sort.

But the party was not as dull as Nanette had anticipated, for Sir Simeon had invited to meet them not only his son and his daughter-in-law but also his three grandsons, who were young, unmarried, and only a few years older than Nanette.

She therefore laughed and flirted with them while Prunella listened to the old Judge reminiscing about her father and how much they had enjoyed themselves when they had been undergraduates at Oxford together.

There was more shopping to do in the afternoon, and when it was nearly time to dress for dinner, Prunella expected Nanette to tell her some lie to enable her to meet Pascoe.

Instead she said:

"I have a headache, Prunella, and I am going to bed early. Can we have dinner at seven o'clock?"

"Of course, dearest, and it would be wise for us all, including Charity, to have an early night, as we have a long drive in front of us tomorrow."

After a light meal in their Sitting-Room, Nanette said to Prunella:

"I am sorry if you are angry with me and I have disappointed you. I know that you have always loved me and tried in a way to take Mama's place, and I am grateful, I am really!"

Prunella was so touched that she felt the tears come into her eyes.

"I love you, Nanette," she said, "and everything I do is because I want you to be happy."

"I know that," Nanette answered, "and I love you too."

She kissed Prunella and went to her own bedroom.

Prunella went to hers and when she was undressed and in bed she told herself that she had been right in thinking that Nanette had communicated with Pascoe.

She would have told him she was going to Bath and he had doubtless replied that he would follow her.

"That fortune-hunting young man will get a

surprise when he cannot find her," Prunella told herself.

Then she wondered what the Earl would think.

Had he really asked her to marry him? She could hardly believe it was true, and yet he had actually said the words.

It suddenly struck her that perhaps being married to the Earl would be as wonderful as his kiss had been.

Then she forced herself not to think of the strange streak of pain which had swept through her and which had changed to an ecstasy that had carried her towards the stars.

"I have to . . . think only of Nanette . . . Nanette . . . Nanette!"

She thought the words were being repeated over and over again in her mind as finally she fell into a restless, disturbed sleep in which she dreamt she was running away from the Earl but could not escape him.

Chapter Seven

Prunella pulled back the curtains from her bed-room window before Charity came to call her.

It was a sunny morning and she had the feeling that she was taking a momentous step into the unknown and she had no idea what would happen in the future.

How could she and Nanette wander about the world simply with the object of avoiding two men?

Then she told herself sharply that she had to do what was right, and that was to prevent Nanette from marrying a fortune-hunter.

She dressed quickly, expecting every moment to hear Charity knock on the door.

She thought perhaps her clock was wrong and remembered that it had been erratic for some time.

When she was dressed she did not stop to admire her new gown in the mirror, but walked briskly through the Sitting-Room towards Nanette's room on the other side of it.

She entered and found the curtains drawn, and to her surprise Charity was sitting in a chair crying.

"What is the matter? What has happened?"

Prunella asked as she looked towards the bed to see that it was empty.

"She's gone — Miss Prunella," Charity sobbed, "and I'll never — forgive myself — never! "

"What are you talking about?" Prunella asked.

Then she saw that lying on the pillow on the bed there was a note.

She opened it, anticipating almost exactly what she would read.

Dearest Prunella,

Forgive me, and I know you will be angry, but Pascoe and I have run away to be married. We are going to France, where Pascoe says there will be no uncomfortable questions asked as to whether I have my Guardian's permission, and we will honeymoon in Paris.

When we return, please, please, forgive me, because I love you.

Nanette

When she had finished reading Prunella stood as if turned to stone. Then she turned towards Charity, saying:

"You knew about this!"

"I should have told you, Miss Prunella, but she'd have gone anyway, and how could you have stopped her with you only in your nightgown?"

Prunella drew in her breath and asked in a quite calm voice:

"At what time did she leave?"

"About seven-o'clock. I heard her moving and came into the room to find her dressed in a travelling-gown ordering a porter to carry down her baggage."

"Seven-o'clock!" Prunella repeated to herself.

She was calculating in her mind how long it would take Nanette and Pascoe to reach Dover.

Then she knew there was only one person who could help her, and that was the Earl.

'He could catch them up,' she thought.

Then, as if she had received a painful blow, she remembered that she did not know where he was.

"Have you any idea, Charity," she asked, "where His Lordship is staying in London?"

"He's at Winslow House, Miss Prunella."

"Winslow House!" Prunella exclaimed incredulously. "How can he be? And how do you know?"

"The footman told me when he brought a note for Miss Nanette every morning. Oh, Miss! You'll never forgive me! I should have told you, but it made her so happy."

Charity's voice was almost incoherent and the tears were streaming down her old face.

Prunella walked from the room back to her own bedroom.

Hastily she put on her bonnet and, picking up her reticule, hurried down the stairs to the vestibule.

"I want a hackney-carriage," she said to the porter, "and tell him to drive me to Winslow

173

House in Berkeley Square."

"Very good, Miss."

There was a hackney-carriage waiting outside and a few minutes later Prunella was on her way.

She found it hard to believe that the Earl was staying in Winslow House, which had been closed ever since the late Earl had felt he was too ill and too old to visit London.

The Earl's Town-House was one thing she had not made her responsibility, and she wondered if there were old servants there who had not been paid, or if the place had become very dilapidated with anyone being aware of it.

Then she told herself sharply that the only person who need concern her now was Nanette.

It was only a short distance to Berkeley Square and when she stepped out of the carriage and rang the bell, the door was opened by a servant who looked surprised at anyone calling so early.

"I wish to see His Lordship!"

"Is His Lordship expecting you, Madam?"

"No, but please tell him Miss Broughton is here and that it is very urgent."

"Will you come this way, Miss?"

She was led across a marble Hall, and servants who, she noted with surprise, were dressed in the Winslow livery, opened the door of what was obviously a Morning-Room.

The furniture was impressive and obviously valuable, and the walls were hung with old masters in gold frames, although the curtains looked faded, as did the brocade on the chairs and the sofa.

'There must be many treasures worth a great deal of money here!' Prunella thought to herself, and wondered if the Earl would sell these as well.

Then the door opened and when he came into the room she could not help a sudden feeling that her heart had turned a somersault.

He looked very smart and impressive and there was that buccaneering, raffish look in his eyes which made her remember, although she tried not to do so, what she had felt when he had kissed her.

"Good-morning, Prunella! You are an early visitor," he remarked.

Prunella forced her voice to sound cold and accusing as she held out Nanette's letter.

"This is your fault!"

The Earl took the letter from her, read it, and said with a smile:

"At least Pascoe is putting up a fight for what he wants!"

"If that is your only comment," Prunella said, "I consider it extremely reprehensible!"

"I knew you would feel angry," the Earl replied, "but they have taken things into their own hands and there is nothing we can do about it."

"There is certainly something I can do!" Prunella retorted, "but I need your help."

"In what way?"

"I am sure it will take them, with the sort of horses Pascoe is likely to be able to afford, at least six hours if not more to reach Dover. I believe, and I think I am not mistaken, that there are usually only two ships to France every day, one in the morning and one in the afternoon."

"So you intend to try to prevent them from catching the afternoon ship?"

"I do!"

"And you wish me to drive you to Dover?"

"I think you could do so far quicker than I could manage with a Post-Chaise, however expensive."

"Very well," the Earl said. "I will order my Phaeton to come to your Hotel in an hour's time."

"Why must I wait an hour?"

"I have certain arrangements to make before I can leave London," the Earl replied. "I also have not yet had my breakfast."

Prunella made an exasperated little sound, but she knew from the way he had spoken that she would gain nothing by arguing with him.

Instead of which she said:

"Very well, I will return to the Hotel and will bring with me a small bag in case Nanette and I have to stay the night."

The Earl's lips curled in a faint smile, but he merely crossed the room to open the door. Only as they reached the Hall did he ask:

"You would not like to wait while I send for my carriage?"

"I shall be waiting impatiently at the Hotel, My Lord," Prunella answered. "As you are well aware, we have to reach Dover before the afternoon ship sails."

"I will not forget," the Earl replied.

The footman fetched a hackney-carriage, and standing on the doorstep, the Earl watched Prunella drive away.

Sitting stiffly upright, she did not bow to him but looked straight ahead, and when she was out of sight the Earl turned back into the Hall and started to give orders.

It was an hour and ten minutes later when the Earl's Phaeton, with a team of perfectly matched chestnuts, drew up outside the Hotel.

On any other occasion Prunella would not only have admired the horses but would also have wondered how he managed to afford them.

But because he was late she was too agitated to think of anything but that they should be on their way and she must reach Dover before Nanette was spirited away to France.

Then there would be no possibility of her preventing her sister from becoming the wife of the man she despised.

Her small case, which had been packed by Charity, was placed at the back of the Phaeton, and Prunella was helped by one of the porters into the seat beside the Earl.

Standing forlornly in the doorway, Charity waved good-bye but received no response from her mistress.

"What am I to do with myself? Where am I to go, Miss Prunella?" she had asked.

"You will wait here with my luggage until I

return, Charity," Prunella replied.

She had said nothing more, and although she longed to reproach Charity for having helped Nanette in being so deceitful, she did not want to upset the old woman.

The Earl drove superbly and she knew it was what she might have expected of him. The horses were fresh and they moved quickly out of London and were soon in the open countryside.

They had driven for quite a long way in silence before Prunella remarked:

"There is certainly not as much traffic as I expected."

"When one is in a hurry it is always wise to avoid the main highways," the Earl replied.

Prunella said no more, for it was difficult to speak when they were moving so fast. She also had no wish to divert the Earl's attention from his horses when time was of such importance.

It was noon when the Earl drew into the yard of a small but attractive Posting-Inn.

"Why are we stopping?" Prunella asked.

"I am hungry," the Earl replied, "and I am sure you are too. Also this is where we change horses."

"You have your own horses here?" Prunella asked in surprise.

"Yes," the Earl replied.

He did not sound as if he wished to be any more communicative, but it flashed through Prunella's mind that it was yet another unnecessary extravagance.

Yet she was well aware that Gentlemen of Fashion kept their own horses at Posting-Inns on all the main roads.

Prunella was taken upstairs to a low oak-beamed bedroom to wash and she took off her bonnet to smooth her hair.

Downstairs again, she was shown into a small private parlour where the Earl was waiting and luncheon, an unexpectedly good one, was served almost immediately.

Because she was so intent on hurrying, Prunella did not argue when the Earl insisted on her having a glass of wine with her meal.

They had eaten for a short while in silence before he said:

"Perhaps I have been remiss in not telling you sooner that you look very lovely today."

She looked at him in surprise because it was a compliment she had not expected, then when her eyes met his, she felt herself blush.

"I have no . . . time to think about . . . myself," she said after a moment.

Her reply was meant to sound cold and impersonal but instead it was low and shy, and she was unable to go on looking at the Earl.

"But I have had time to think about you," he said, "and later, when you are not so agitated, I would like to talk about us — you and me."

"N-no . . . please . . ." Prunella pleaded.

"Why not?" he asked. "After all, although I should like your sister to be happy, I am not really concerned with her but with you."

"It is . . . something you . . . must not be."

"Why?"

"Because I have to look after Nanette . . . and that means that we cannot . . . stay at the Manor . . ."

She broke off what she was saying and gave an exasperated little sound.

"All this has happened because I told her yesterday we were going to Bath and then perhaps to Paris. She must have written to Pascoe immediately, and they plotted together to elope."

"That is exactly what happened."

Prunella looked at the Earl and gave a little cry.

"You knew . . . this was what they were . . . going to . . . do?"

"Shall I say I had a good idea of it?"

"Why did you not prevent them? Why did you not tell me?"

"Because, Prunella," the Earl said, "Pascoe is a man. He must make his own decisions in life, and I would also point out that he is my nephew, not my son."

"At the same time . . . you might have thought . . . of me."

"I did think of you, as it happens, and later I will tell you how much, but now we ought to be on our way."

"Yes, of course," Prunella agreed.

She put on her bonnet and tied it under her chin. As she did so, she told herself that she was very angry with the Earl for not having taken a more positive attitude towards the run-aways.

But somehow the hatred she had been able to feel about him in the past was no longer there.

Instead she could only think of the expression in his eyes and the faint smile on his lips — lips which had kissed hers.

The Earl's fresh team of the fittest bays seemed to move as quickly as, if not quicker than, the chestnuts.

'How can he possess such marvellous animals?' Prunella wondered.

They were moving too quickly to ask questions, and time passed before, driving down a narrow, empty road, the Earl suddenly drew the bays to a standstill under the shade of a great chestnut tree.

Prunella looked at him in surprise.

"Why are we stopping?"

"There is something I want to tell you."

There was a note in the Earl's voice that made her look up at him apprehensively.

He transferred the reins to his right hand and turned in his seat so that he was facing her.

"You think we are on our way to Dover," he said quietly, "but actually we have less than two hours' driving before we reach home."

For a moment Prunella felt that she could not have heard him aright.

"H-home?" she faltered.

"Your home and mine," the Earl said. "The Hall!"

"But I want to go to Dover . . . and Nanette! How dare you not . . . take me there as you . . . promised!"

"I did not promise anything," the Earl replied. "You gave me your orders and you assumed I was obeying you."

"I have to stop Nanette!" Prunella cried almost wildly.

"If you were able to do so, it would be, I think, a great mistake."

"How can you say such a thing?"

"I am saying it because I believe in all sincerity that Nanette and my nephew Pascoe are well suited to each other. They will have to struggle to put Pascoe's Estate in order, just as they have had to struggle to get married, and I think it will be very good for both of them."

"You do not know what you are . . . saying!"

"I do know," the Earl answered. "Just as I know what is best for you, my darling, even though you may not agree with me."

Despite her bewilderment, because of the depth of feeling in his voice she felt a little quiver go through her.

"What is more," the Earl went on, "we are on our way home, but as I cannot take you to the Hall without a Chaperone, I have decided that we must first be married."

"Married . . . ?"

Prunella could barely say the word.

"Half-a-mile from here," the Earl continued, "there is a Church where a Parson is waiting for us. It is no use raging at me, Prunella. I love you, and although you may deny it, I know you love me. I have a Special Licence and we are going to be married at once."

For a moment Prunella was speechless, but then as the Earl waited she found her voice.

"Of course I . . . will not . . . marry you! How can you . . . think of . . . such . . . a thing?"

The Earl reached out his left hand and put his fingers under Prunella's chin to turn her face up to his.

"Look at me, my sweet, look me in the eyes and tell me, by everything you hold sacred, that you do not love me and that when I kissed you it meant nothing to you except to increase the dislike and contempt you have expressed so often before."

Prunella wanted to struggle against him but somehow it was impossible to do so.

His fingers held her chin firmly, and despite herself her eyes met his.

Then she could not look away or struggle any more.

Instead, she felt as if the whole world vanished and there was nothing but his eyes and a strange, unaccountable ecstasy rising within her as it had done the night he had kissed her.

For a long, long moment neither of them could move. Then the Earl said very quietly:

"You are mine, my precious, as I always meant you to be!"

He released her and drove on.

Utterly bemused and feeling as if the whole world had turned upside-down, Prunella could not move until she saw just ahead of them a small grey-stone Church, and standing at the lych-gate was a man she recognised as Jim.

As the Earl drew up his horses he ran to their heads.

Prunella sat still until the Earl reached her side of the Phaeton and helped her to the ground.

Then, although she did not intend it to happen, her fingers held on to his as if he gave her the strength she needed.

"You . . . really . . . mean to do . . . this?" she asked in a whisper.

"I mean to make you my wife," he replied.

He put her hand on his arm, then covered it with his.

She found that her will had left her, and, no longer able to think what she should or should not do, she felt utterly subservient to him.

He led her down the small path and in through the door of the Church.

It was very old and quiet and their footsteps seemed to ring out on the flagged floor as they walked up the aisle to where at the Chancel steps a Parson, wearing a white surplice, was waiting for them.

Afterwards Prunella could only think that a stranger had taken possession of her body, a stranger had spoken her responses in the Marriage Service, a stranger had knelt beside the Earl after the Parson had declared them man and wife and blessed them.

Then, without speaking to each other, without saying a word, they walked back through the sunlit Church-yard. Jim released the horses' heads and they were driving on.

It was after a short while that Prunella began to recognise the countryside and wonder how she had been so foolish as to be deceived into thinking they were going to Dover instead of . . . home.

She felt the word meant something different from what it had ever meant before, because it was not to the Manor the Earl was taking her, but to the Hall.

She thought too that she must have all her life dreamt, although she had never put it into words, that it would one day be hers, and she would love it and tend it and somehow, in a way which seemed impossible, she would restore it to its former glory.

Although she was thinking of the Earl's house, at the same time she was acutely conscious that he was beside her; that he was a man whose name she now bore, that he had kissed her and had said he loved her.

She knew he had been right when he had claimed she loved him too, even though she had tried to fight against it.

He had taken her heart from between her lips and made it his, and even before that she had loved him, although she would rather have died than admit it.

It was her love that made her hate London and miss being with him in the country; and it was love that had made her want to hear his voice and see the smile on his lips and that strange glint in his eyes when he looked at her.

"I love him!" she told herself. "But he had no . . . right to . . . marry me like . . . this!"

It was, however, only her mind that was protesting, because it was conventional to do so.

She knew there was a strange singing in her heart and a feeling of rapture that increased every time she glanced at him out of the corner of her eye.

Then at last, far quicker than she had expected, there were the familiar woods, the undulating countryside, and the small hamlets which she knew were only a few miles from Little Stodbury.

They passed the village Green, then the lane which led to the Manor, and were driving through the stone lodges with the open gates. The great house lay ahead, its windows glittering in the afternoon sun, which was turning to gold.

The Earl drew up his horses with a flourish outside the wide stone steps.

As if they had been waiting for him, two Indian servants stood in the doorway. The Earl handed his reins to a groom, then went round to the other side of the Phaeton.

Prunella put out her hand so that he could

help her alight, but to her surprise he lifted her down; then, carrying her in his arms, he walked up the steps and in through the front door.

Then as he set her down on her feet in the great Hall with its curving staircase he said quietly:

"Welcome home, my darling!"

The way he spoke made her feel almost as if he had kissed her, and because she was shy she turned towards the staircase.

"You will find the Queen's Bedroom has been prepared for you," the Earl said.

Prunella's eyes widened in astonishment.

She wanted to ask him how it could be prepared, how they knew she was to be married. But the servants were listening, so instead she went up the stairs, feeling as if she were moving in a dream from which it was impossible to awaken.

She knew the Queen's Bedroom well, and she loved it. It was one of the State-Rooms she had kept clean and open because it was so beautiful.

It adjoined what was always known as the Master Suite and the windows overlooked both the lake and the rose-garden.

She opened the door and saw to her astonishment that the room, with its huge four-poster bed carved with cupids and draped with blue silk, was not empty.

Charity was there, unpacking her trunks, which lay open on the floor.

"Charity!" Prunella exclaimed.

The old woman rose from the ground to say:

"You're surprised to see me, Miss Prunella? Or rather I should say 'My Lady'!"

Prunella looked at her in bewilderment.

"You . . . know . . . ? How did . . . you know?"

"As soon as you left, His Lordship's servants arrived with a travelling-carriage drawn by six horses. Think of that, M'Lady! Never in m' life have I travelled with six horses, until now!"

"Charity . . . Charity! I do not know what to say," Prunella said.

"There's no point in talking when you should be changing," Charity said sharply in the tone she had used to Prunella when she was a small girl. "Come along now and get out of that dusty gown and into one of your pretty ones, or we'll have His Lordship wishing he had married someone else!"

Prunella gave a weak little laugh that was somehow not very far from tears.

How could this be happening to her? How could she be here in the Queen's Bedroom, with Charity calling her "My Lady"?

They had arrived later than she had thought, and while Charity was helping her out of her gown, a message came from the Earl to say that she should rest until dinner, which would be at seven-thirty.

"Now that's what I call sensible!" Charity said with approval. "You can do with a rest, M'Lady, after having been up half last night a-worrying over Miss Nanette."

"I am still very worried about her," Prunella replied. "Oh, Charity, she ought never to have run away to France to marry Mr. Lowes!"

There was silence for a moment. Then Charity said:

"I know you'll not believe me, M'Lady, but if ever I saw two people truly in love with each other, it was Miss Nanette and His Lordship's nephew."

"She loves him, I grant you that," Prunella said.

"And he loves her. I'd stake my hope of Heaven on it, and that's the truth, Miss — I mean, M'Lady."

"Do you really think so, Charity?"

"Would I be telling you a lie, and would I not want the happiness of my baby?"

There was no answering this, and Prunella allowed herself to be helped into bed, and as Charity pulled the curtains she shut her eyes.

She had the feeling that when she awoke she would find she really had been dreaming and she would not be at the Hall but in her own ordinary little bed at the Manor.

But it was not the Hall or the Manor that she thought of as she fell asleep, but the Earl's eyes looking into hers. . . .

Dinner was finished and it had been a meal with strange, inexplicable silences, interspersed with laughter and moments of shyness when Prunella found it impossible to meet her husband's eyes.

She was vividly conscious of him looking raffish and at the same time extremely elegant in his new evening-clothes.

She was aware that the Indian servants had brought out the finest Winslow silver to decorate the Dining-Room table.

The candles illuminated them both with a golden glow and Prunella felt as if they were taking part in a play in which she was playing the lead part but was not certain how the third act ended.

The servants withdrew soft-footed from the room and Prunella asked:

"What did you do in India?"

It was after a pause which was so pregnant that she felt he must hear her heart beating.

"I worked."

"Worked?"

"I will tell you all about it sometime, but at the moment I can think only of you."

The way he spoke made Prunella blush, and he thought it the loveliest thing he had ever seen.

"You are so young, my darling," he said softly, "so sweet and untouched that I did not believe anyone like you existed today in this blasé, sophisticated world."

"That is the . . . world you . . . know and like," Prunella replied. "I am afraid you will find me . . . very boring."

"It will excite me more than I can tell you to teach you about the things which interest me."

He saw the question in Prunella's eyes and added:

"Which, as far as you are concerned, my beautiful wife, is love."

As Prunella blushed again he rose to his feet.

"You do not wish me to leave you to your port?" she asked.

"I have no wish for any port, nor for you to leave me now or ever!" he replied. "Come, I have something to show you."

He put out his hand and when she took it he felt her fingers tremble in his.

He drew her from the Dining-Room along the corridor, through the Hall, and up the staircase.

The direction in which he turned when they reached the landing told Prunella where they were going, and she felt a sudden impulse to beg him not to spoil the enchantment of their first evening together.

She felt he was going to show her the Picture-Gallery and explain why he had sold the Van Dykes and ask her to forgive him for having done so.

'I shall have to say that I . . . understand . . . and it does not . . . matter,' she thought to herself.

Although she was unaware of it, her fingers stiffened in his and her whole body was tense.

The door of the Picture-Gallery was closed, and as the Earl put out his hand, Prunella wanted to shut her eyes and refuse to look.

Why must he do this to her on their first night

together at the Hall?

Why must he spoil what she had known at dinner was a happiness that seemed to vibrate between them and which deepened until she knew it was the love she felt for him.

A love which she could not prevent from growing every second that she was with him.

"This is what I want to show you, my darling," the Earl said.

Reluctantly, wishing she could run away, Prunella forced herself to look.

For a moment she thought she must have come to the wrong place and that she was not seeing the Picture-Gallery but part of the house she had never been in before.

Then she gave an audible little gasp and knew that as she stared ahead the Earl was watching her face with a smile on his lips.

The three great chandeliers hanging from the ceiling were ablaze with lighted candles and they revealed that the walls which Prunella had last seen empty and dingy with the dust of years had been painted an exquisite shade of red, which was a perfect background for the Van Dykes in their gold frames.

It was the colour which had originally, Prunella knew from the sketches, been chosen by Inigo Jones himself.

The friezes, pediments, and cornices were white picked out in gold, and the curtains which draped the windows were of gold and white brocade.

The paintings in such a setting seemed each to glow like a precious jewel and she could only stand staring, feeling it was not real.

"This is one of my presents to you, my precious one," the Earl said softly.

She turned to look at him, and somehow, she was not certain how it happened, his arms were round her.

"I . . . I do not . . . understand . . . how could you have . . . done this? How could you have . . . made it so perfect?"

"It was done very quickly to please you," he said, "and together you and I will do the rest of the house and restore it to its former glory."

"But how can . . . you? How is . . . it possible?" Prunella stammered.

"What you are really asking is how could I afford it!"

He turned her face up to his.

"Why did you not trust me? Why were you so determined, from the very first moment you met me, that I was a scallywag without a penny to my name?"

"I . . . I thought that you had . . . come to the Hall . . . to find something to . . . s-sell," Prunella whispered.

"And when you saw me looking at the Van Dykes you jumped to the conclusion that I intended to dispose of them."

"You do not . . . have to do . . . so?"

The Earl smiled.

"I happen to be a very rich man, my darling,

with more than enough money for both of us without having to marry you for your fortune."

"I . . . I never suspected . . . you were doing . . . that."

"Yes, I know," he said, "but you believed that I was prepared to throw away my family heir-looms for the horses and for the amusements I would find in London."

Prunella hid her face against his shoulder.

"Forgive . . . me," she whispered.

His arms tightened round her and he said:

"I will forgive you only if you promise not to berate me for crimes I have not committed, or even for those I have."

"I . . . promise . . ."

The words were barely audible but he heard them, and he gave a little laugh before he said:

"I think now that you should thank me for my first wedding-present. I have another for you in my bedroom, and several will be arriving from London within the course of a few days, but perhaps this is the most important."

Prunella raised her head slowly; then, almost before she expected it, the Earl's lips were on hers.

She felt the hard insistence of them, and although she did not try to oppose him or to struggle against him, she was not prepared for the manner in which, without even thinking about it, her mouth surrendered itself to his and her body seemed to melt into his body.

His lips became more passionate and more demanding, then the streak of pain that became a rapture seemed to flash between them, filling her with that wild, unaccountable ecstasy which made her feel that he carried her towards the stars.

'This is love!' she thought.

A love so powerful, so irresistible, so utterly and completely wonderful that nothing else in the whole world mattered or was of any consequence.

Just for one moment she thought that if he offered her a choice between such a wonder and happiness or the possession of every Van Dyke ever painted, she knew which she would take.

It was love she wanted, his love, and him, and no paintings, money, or anything else in the world were of any consequence.

"I love . . . you!" she said, first in her heart, then a little incoherently as the Earl raised his head.

"And I love you, my precious, darling little prude! You beguile me, you intrigue and entrance me, as you have done ever since I first saw you looking at me with such condemnation in your eyes."

"You must . . . have been . . . laughing at me."

"Not laughing, but loving you," he continued, "because you are everything I have sought all over the world but never expected to find."

"Is that . . . true?"

"How could I do anything else but love you, my lovely one, not only for your beauty but because in every way you are the opposite of what I have been myself."

"It does not . . . matter what . . . you have . . . been."

"Do you mean that?"

She looked up at him and he could see the truth shining in her eyes.

"I . . . love you . . . just as you are . . . and you are right . . . love is . . . irresistible and very . . . very wonderful!"

She saw the smile that came to his lips before he pulled her closer to him.

Then he was kissing her again; kissing her until the Picture-Gallery whirled round them and there was nothing but themselves and a starlit sky.

What they owned, precious and divine, was the treasure all men and women seek — the love which cannot be bought but only given by God.

The employees of G.K. Hall hope you have enjoyed this Large Print book. All our Large Print titles are designed for easy reading, and all our books are made to last. Other G.K. Hall books are available at your library, through selected bookstores, or directly from us.

For information about titles, please call:

(800) 223-1244
(800) 223-6121

To share your comments, please write:

Publisher
G.K. Hall & Co.
295 Kennedy Memorial Drive
Waterville, ME 04901